SECOND EDITION

Call Out The Dolphins

A Collection of Short Stories and Verse

Chris S. Buckley

CALL OUT THE DOLPHINS
A COLLECTION OF SHORT STORIES AND VERSE

iUniverse books may be ordered through booksellers or by contacting:

iUniverse
1663 Liberty Drive
Bloomington, IN 47403
www.iuniverse.com
1-800-Authors (1-800-288-4677)

ISBN: 978-1-5320-8929-9 (sc)
ISBN: 978-1-5320-8930-5 (e)

Print information available on the last page.

iUniverse rev. date: 11/25/2019

For Cali

Contents

Foreword

The year is 1962. JFK is in the White House; the Giants and Yankees are in the World Series; rock and roll is redefining itself, and a pre-pubescent kid walks alone at night, through the 'burbs of Home Town. A bright green pouch hangs from his belt. Coins which have found their way through wads of paper dollars, to the bottom of the pouch, jingle with every step. The pouch is labeled with a newspaper logo, but probably should read "I am twelve years old, defenseless, and in possession of large amounts of cash. Please rob me."

I only got mugged once. Not at night, but in bold daylight, by two guys, a couple years older and much bigger than I, one of whom would, years later, become the captain of the high school football team. He held me while his goon-in-training hit me. When the hitter reached for my cash stuffed pouch, I kicked for all I was worth and landed it squarely to his groin. Then, on the back swing, my heel caught the future football star's shin, and I was free.

As I made my fleet footed escape, I decided Mom and Dad didn't need to know about this. They'd only make me quit the paper route, my first job, and probably scold me for having allowed the botched robbery to take place. They could be overprotective, and a job that threatened my physical wellness or indeed my life, would certainly not be an option.

Fast forward to the 2010s. It's about noon on California's Lost Coast, where an inevitable death has occurred. You won't hear about it on the radio, see it on TV or the internet, or even read about it, in a soon to be extinct newspaper. In attendance at the memorial service, maybe sixty feet from the freeway, under a towering oak tree, are only two people. The grave digger and the dear departed's dearly beloved, me.

To understand the connection between the body in the grave and the sole mourner, we'll have to go back about thirteen years. She was on death row in the county lock-up, booked on a charge of vagrancy. She was a trusting sort. It'd been her nature since birth, so when the uniform with a shiny badge told her that he was her friend, she naturally believed him. She'd soon find that she had that gullibility issue in common with yours truly, who himself had landed in hot water more than once, taken in by carefully constructed, counterfeit sincerities. What we also have in common is that neither of us ever stopped trusting, a trait that could have doubled as a death sentence for the girl in the grave. But, for me? Who knows? Out of four billion people wandering the planet, surely there's one who'll choose *not* to abuse the gift of trust, in favor of a predictable need to line their coffers.

Meanwhile, back on death row, a month or so had passed. There'd been lots of lookers, but no takers. With no one to claim the shiny haired orphan, her time was growing short. Her cell seemed to get closer by the day to the gas chamber door, something which turned out not to be her imagination. For every day that she wasn't claimed, she'd get a new cell, just like the old one, but closer to 'the door.' By the time I arrived, her insight to human nature had become honed to the point of a keen sense of what would or would not impress potential sponsors. As I strolled past the cells, all the homeless, doomed criminals would stand, one after the other, to show themselves off, as they added a little vocalizing, which, regardless of what it sounded like, always came out as, "Take me! Take me!"

When I got to the quarters of our little girl lost, she decided, based on the life experience she must've seen etched into my face, that I could probably appreciate her making the best of a bad situation. With that, she stretched out on a makeshift bed, and appeared as contented as circumstances would allow. It worked. Within three days, we shared my roof. Just her and me, for all of her remaining years.

The casket is just a cardboard box, sealed with duct tape. Poor girl didn't rate a fancy coffin, with frills and a hinged lid. Cats seldom do.

What, then, you may ask, is the connection between a bullied paperboy in 1962, and a dead cat, some fifty years later? With the burial of the cat – her name was Trudy, by the by – I also buried a fifty year long string of jobs, which began with, you guessed it, a paper route. Jobs that would occupy my time, as I waited patiently to be noticed, whether musically, theatrically, literarily or cinematically. This was a storytelling need that first presented itself when your long winded narrator, at the age of seven, witnessed an eighteen foot tall teenage werewolf, who jumped off a big grey screen, and into my nightmares.

Think of me as the Little Big Man of the work force. I've partied with bigoted rednecks, caucused with revolutionaries, rubbed friendly elbows with the vein and superficial, all the while, having befriended at least one from each encampment. If nothing else, we had our employer in common. Like the Dustin Hoffman character, amid my apparent adaptability that improved with every job, are the occasional pearls of wisdom or ignorance left to me by all those fellow toilers, each of which would take its place as a lesson, good or bad, not soon forgotten.

There are three essential elements to all things tangible or imagined. They are the beginning, the middle and the end. The best example of this claim, from where I sit, is anything that happens to be alive. Like a play or a movie, our lifetimes unfold in three acts. Act one, the 'Who is he? What does he want? Who's going to stop him?' act is far behind us and we're about to wrap act two, the longest of the trio, where our protagonist found, in pursuit of his happiness, it isn't always *who* wants to stop him, but *what.* After a brief intermission, he'll take his place and the curtain will rise for act three. At this point, we only hope for survival. That now qualifies as happiness. And a favorable review wouldn't hurt.

Short stories and short films have one common advantage over the longer or feature length versions: If you don't like the story, take heart: it'll be over soon. The same can be said of verse. Accordingly, your tour guide for today presents a parade of randomly chosen stories and verse, in no particular order. Some fact, some fiction, some fact-based fiction, which, mercifully, will all be over soon. Lest I forget, have a pleasant flight!

Until the Afterward,

Chris B.

The Epiphany

Jonathon Briggs' first brush with religious conflict came at an early age. He was about five. An only child, he spent most of his daylight hours next door, with Bobby Soxer, a year older than Jonathon, and all of Bobby's siblings. The Soxers were a wholesome Catholic family of seven who, according to Bobby, were privi to have Lucifer himself -- the actual anti-Christ -- residing directly under their house. This, for Jonathon, would begin a lifetime of easily targeted gullibility.

Bobby had more news, and it wasn't good. Seems Jonathon, or rather his soul, would be going to hell, under Bobby's house, when he dies, to suffer eternal damnation, at the hands of Lucifer and his pitchfork, because he wasn't Catholic. Only Catholics could get into Heaven. Bobby knew this to be factual, as the nuns at All Saints School had assured him of it, and if it came from a nun, it must be true. Logically, Jonathon's life choices added up to only one: Try not to die. He was very careful to steer clear of potentially harmful situations, serving a lot of time under his bed, with the dust bunnies and dirty underwear.

One afternoon, not long after Jonathon was alerted to the eternal damnation that awaited him, he and Bobby engaged in a standoff. Bobby stood near the left headlight of his grandfather's Rambler, Jonathon, or 'Jonny,' near the right. They'd fought every day at about this time, and Bobby had always won. It was a necessary link in the pecking order. Bobby's older brother would beat him up. He, in turn, would beat up Jonny, and, if the beating didn't send him home, crying and swearing he'd never go back, Jonny'd beat up Bobby's little brother, Oscar.

But this day would violate tradition. This day, Jonny wielded a weapon. A coffee can. With full knowledge of Jonathon's winless back yard tussle record, Bobby taunted him, sporting no weapons, save for a smug little grin and a clenched fist.

"Go ahead, Jonny," Bobby goaded, "throw it at me. If you don't, I'll just have to beat you up, anyway. And if you do--"

He pointed over his shoulder, toward the ground level double door that led under the Soxer house, aka the doorway to hell. Bobby was right. These two options, get beat up or go to hell, didn't add up to much. With that in mind, Jonathon decided he'd get his money's worth, and thusly, gave the can a casual, underhanded fling toward his sole aggressor.

A direct hit to the forehead, and the Goliath who'd taunted Jonathon, dropped like a felled tree. Jonny ran to him and gazed, horrified, at what he'd done. After a brief glance at Mephistopheles' doorway, believing he'd killed his friend, Jonny ran home to the safe haven under his bed.

Fate smiled upon Jonathon, as he hadn't actually killed Bobby, just knocked him out. That night, Bobby's mother would call to demand an apology, something Jonny was only too happy to run over and deliver.

Decades later, Jonathon, now a confirmed, but tolerant non-believer, made a comfortable living as a bartender, in a golf course clubhouse. Among his regular, golf addicted clientele were three priests, Fathers Mac, Doolittle and Brady, who, once weekly, usually Wednesday, would play eighteen holes, in street clothes, and finished the day at Jonathon's bar, tabulating their scores. Fathers Mac and Brady drank Old Fashions and scotch/rocks, respectively, while Father Doolittle, a recovering alcoholic, originally from the Midwest, enjoyed a plain Bloody Mary mix. He was always careful not to request it by its traditional recipe name, a Virgin Mary. Jonathon, however, wasn't quite so bound by divine censorship.

"Gonna have a virgin today, Father?"

"Oh, you betcha."

A typical night during Jonny's tenure at the golf course would find him on the homebound freeway by 10 or 11pm. He could take the freeway north or south. Either way, he'd eventually find his way home. North was the more prudent direction, as it was all freeway, to Jonny's front door. South was the long way, past and usually *into* at least five bars, where he'd drop the lion's share of the day's tips. Most of the bartenders knew him, thus he could be assured that the over-tips he left them would find their way back to him when they visited his plank. 'Musical money' is a polite term for the process. True insiders may know it as honor among thieves.

Safe at home by 2:30am or thereabouts, Jonathon still wasn't yet ready to call it a wrap, and wouldn't be until after a few more nightcaps. With bottle and glass in hand, he'd find his way back out the front door of his humble abode, then back into his compact station wagon, which, after a long since repossessed Mercury, had been like driving a sewing machine. But this car had all that Jonny really cared about. FM. The plan? To drink wine, smoke cigarettes, and listen to an eclectic music radio station, with progressive country leanings, until he passed out, all behind the wheel of his parked sewing machine.

On one such night, the eclectic music radio station eventually lulled Jonathon to sleep with an Emmy Lou Harris ballad. He was awakened a short time later by an icy mist that blanketed his face. No longer behind the wheel of the compact station wagon, he now found himself in the back seat of a '56 Cadillac convertible, top down. The big car was was rocketing northerly, *way* northerly, into the clouds. The mist was freezing Jonny's face, though he didn't seem to mind. Had he died in his sleep? Should he be in a panic?

Seated to Jonathon's left was Elvis. He looked good. Young, vibrant and ready to rock, as he had been, the year this Cadillac was manufactured. When Jonny told him he liked him in King Creole, he said "Thank you very much."

Seated quietly on Elvis' left was a Pope, fully robed and capped. Which Pope is anybody's guess, as they all tend to look alike. Appropriately enough, their chauffeur, according to his posted hack license, was none other than St. Peter, storied liaison between the Pope and you-know-who.

As the four wheeled guided missile soared silently through the clouds, Jonny engaged Elvis in some chit chat to pass the time, "I thought you died years ago, so, just curious, what's the delay?"

"Aw, you know, paperwork, appeals. The big guy didn't like me messin' around with those nurses in rehab. But you, sir. Wow, they fast tracked you right on into the kingdom. I'm a little confused about that, but it's still an honor and a privilege to ride by your side, sir."

"Yeah, I'm a little confused, I -- Uh, thanks. Likewise, I'm sure,"

"Thank you very much."

Pete broke out some burgers and the contented passengers all munched while they chatted. The burger was the best Jonny'd ever eaten. Elvis and the Pope agreed that they were cooked perfectly, with all the right garnishes. Pete was glad they liked them, as burgers are "Kind of a delicacy up here because we have to wait for the cows to die, naturally."

Jonathon's two ride mates were quite interested in hearing about his varietal array of jobs, and the simple lifestyle he'd chosen. He'd never thought of his life as simple, but supposed, in comparison to theirs, any lifestyle would appear uncomplicated.

Uncomplicated was what Elvis and the Pope had both secretly wished for during their time on Earth. But then, neither of them ever had to build a resume or concoct a believable reason for leaving his last job. Neither could have anonymously wandered through a museum, amid a curious crowd of spectators. Neither could have spontaneously decided to go to a ballgame or take a drive in the country on a warm night. All this sounded pretty good to the pontiff and the king. While neither seemed to have any regrets, for the first time ever, nor did Jonny.

The airborne Caddy coasted to a stop at the fabled pearly gates.

Pete reached out and punched a few buttons on a keypad. The gates opened and the big Caddy glided through. A few twists and turns on a road that didn't exist, and they arrived at an unpretentious little cottage, with a small, well kept yard, white picket fence and a mailbox. The Pope bade farewell to Jonny and the others as he exited the car.

Next stop, another little cottage, not unlike the Pope's. This would be Elvis' new digs. As he got out of the car, Jonathon told him he enjoyed their chat. Elvis said "Thank you very much." Jonny couldn't help noticing, as he and Pete glided off, that Elvis' mother greeted him at the front door of the small house. Who else? He sure was glad to see her.

A few clouds up the road, Peter stopped the Caddy in front of a sprawling mansion. Jonathon assumed this was 'the big guy's place' until Pete got out of the car and, like any dutiful chauffeur, opened Jonny's door for him to exit.

"And this is your new home, for all eternity, my friend," Pete said as he motioned toward the huge estate.

Jonathon guardedly vacated the limo, his gaze fixed on the vastness of the mansion and its surrounding grounds, with pillars that stretched so high, he couldn't see where they ended. A chorus of angels, off to their left, sang another Emmy Lou Harris song. Maybe it was Linda Ronstadt. Regardless, there was something seriously wrong with this picture. Or so believed our protagonist.

Jonny had to inquire, "Wait. Are you sure you got the directions right? Shouldn't Elvis and the Pope be living here? And shouldn't I be in one of those cottages?"

"Nooo," Peter quickly responded, "Popes and do-gooders are a dime a dozen up here. We get 'em by the carload. But you're the first bartender who ever made it. Now *that's* cause for rejoicing."

"What? You mean out of all those millions of bartenders -- well, where'd they go?"

Sadness befell St. Peter. Suddenly it dawned on Jonathon, "You don't mean--"

Pete nodded, slowly, then lamented, "Under Bobby's house."

Old Howard and the Lost Children

Rhett and Snider, friends since childhood, now in their late teens, were dispatched to a poultry farm by an experimental community outreach program for "Youth Between Jobs." Their qualifications, according to the program's guidelines, were emphatically stellar. They were terminally unemployed.

At the farm, they were interviewed, tested and sent to a country doctor for a physical. The two teens were then dispatched to their respective departments for another interview. Why all the tests and interviews for a minimum wage job? It's not like they'd applied for top secret government positions. Or was it? They assumed they'd be feeding chickens and collecting eggs, but Snider was assigned to inter-departmental pick up and delivery, while Rhett's new job title would be that of lab assistant.

Rhett's immediate supervisor, a guy named Garth, who always wore a lab coat, actually *looked* like a chicken. With a marked widow's peak that pointed down to a thin face and hooked nose, Rhett surmised Garth had surely been a rooster in another life. Unlike most roosters, however, he was a good natured sort, with a sense of humor and a taste for coffee, by the gallon. Garth's superior, and director of the lab, was a soft spoken, older man, Dr. Dotter, a celebrated veterinarian, who'd left a lucrative practice, to oversee this enterprise.

Garth patiently walked Rhett through his duties, all of which he'd demonstrate, then have Rhett try, once. He did fine with everything -- hosing down floors, sorting dead birds for autopsy, packing eggs for shipment to other labs. Then, however, they got to the death chamber.

"No, you don't wring their necks. That takes all day, it's messy and your arm gets tired," Garth instructed, "Just hold its legs like this."

He grabbed the live chicken's legs, held it upside down, then continued, while demonstrating, "And with your other hand, hold the back of its head between your forefinger and index finger, like this, and just one flick of the wrist, outward."

Rhett heard the snap of the chicken's neck. Its wings flapped violently, so signaling instant death. Garth tossed it across the room, onto a pile of carcasses, picked up another live chicken by its legs and held it out to Rhett, "Now you try it."

"That's okay, I'm sure I'll know how, when the time –"

"No, I want you to do this. You'll be doing a lot of it. We kill a lot of birds here, so I need to know now if you can handle it."

Reluctantly, Rhett followed his directions, to the letter. The bird's neck snapped, wings flailed, and he'd become another chicken terminator.

The executioner's lesson wouldn't end there. Garth showed Rhett into the brooder house. The warmth, the sound of a thousand babies, chirping for their mothers, and especially the smell, took him back to simpler times. His dad, all those years ago, bought a broken down, but functional incubator, and they innocently raised chicks into chickens, but only for the eggs.

One of the chicks had escaped its brooder, and ran around, in a panicked state, on the floor. The chick appeared and sounded like just what it was, a lost child. Garth picked it up, looked it over. The baby bird seemed to trust him, as it stopped chirping and looked up into his chicken face, like an adoring child. He would surely help the fuzzy newborn back to the security of its incubator.

"This little guy earned himself an early exit, I'm afraid," Garth said.

"How do you know which brooder to put him back in?"

"Oh, he can't go back. Might infect the other birds from the droppings on his feet."

He carried the chick -- the kind you might see in fabric softener commercials -- over to a nearby table, as he continued, "The chicks are easier to kill. You just press their little necks against the edge of a table, with your thumb, until they snap. Like this."

True to his expert instruction, with just his thumb, Garth pressed the life out of the newborn in one short motion, then tossed it into a nearby garbage can. Rhett silently gave more serious thought to the virtues of becoming a full time college student. Maybe there was still time. In honor of the dollar, however, he'd bear up under the pressures of morality and, after a few weeks, be breaking necks, scissoring up carcasses by the dozen, and bagging the occasionally decomposed remains, all concurrent with the guilt meter's fleet fade to black. This, however, will be the year of Rhett's first far reaching affirmation, and the chickens will help.

The incubator babies had all been injected with various growth hormones at birth. The medications would increase their size and the speed at which they reached it. After about a week, they'd be moved to the 'Hill House,' far from the main ranch. Rhett wondered why, as he and Garth traveled by car, up the curvy dirt road, the birds had to be so sequestered. His answer waited at the end of their dusty ride.

Stepping into Hill House was like stepping into a low budget 1950s science fiction movie. Through the chain link gate labeled AUTHORIZED PERSONELL ONLY, then into the feed room, where Rhett was introduced to Paul, a tender whose only job it was to tend this single house.

After glancing at the sign on the next door, GOWNS AND MASKS ONLY BEYOND THIS POINT, Garth had to ask, "Are the chickens radioactive?" A little levity, most unappreciated.

The chickens, known in the vernacular as pullets, barely out of infancy, were the size of turkeys, and not yet even fully feathered. Quite clumsy and uncoordinated because their baby brains hadn't yet learned how to maneuver the mammoth legs, they'd take a few steps, then stumble or fall over.

"What'll happen to them now?" Rhett asked, still a bit shocked by the site of them.

"They'll reach maturity, then most of 'em will die of heart attacks. These are good eating, by the way. I've barbecued a few myself. Lotta fat, though."

Was that a joke? If so, Rhett didn't laugh. They were even.

Apart from new and better ways to fatten chickens up for market, there loomed another more serious research issue being dealt with by Dr. Dotter & Co.

"Mareks disease," Garth explained, "is an incurable, contagious, airborne viral infection. It cripples and blinds the bird, paralyzing its neck and, like a cancer, it produces huge internal tumors. No known cure."

If a sick bird, displaying the obvious symptoms, was brought into the lab, Rhett's instructions were to kill it immediately and place it in the pile, on the cement floor, to be autopsied. Usually no need for the executioner's ritual, however, as the majority of incoming were DOA.

On a particular hot afternoon, burned into Rhett's memory for this, and perhaps all time, not because of the heat, but because of an exchange with yet another soft spoken, 60ish gentleman, there took place an encounter we'll call *part one* of the affirmation.

'Old Howard' they called him, though never in his presence. Then it was just Howard. Rhett liked him from the start, as everyone did. After being introduced in passing, Garth told Rhett that Howard had been a tender on the ranch for forty years, in the same house, and had never missed a day of work. An exaggeration? If you knew Howard, you knew it wasn't. His house, according to Garth, was always the cleanest, his hens, the top producers. Rhett envied Howard's obvious inner peace and his genuine cheerfulness, as he wondered how long he'd have to wait to find that same peace, if ever. We all want to be appreciated. It seems those who care the least about that ego-propelled concept, like Old Howard, are always the runaway prize winners.

This day, up to about three o'clock, was not unlike any other. Rhett's routines, by now, had become second nature, mostly carried out subconsciously, while right-brain daydreams of everything from success laden scenarios to skinny dipping in the company lake with the cute blond girl who worked in the front office, filed through the forefront of his consciousness, like a passing parade. He'd only seen her a few times, from a distance, but she always waved and smiled sweetly, as though they'd been old friends. Or maybe something more.

Rhett had a good sized row of birds prepared for autopsy, all of which were laid on their backs, side by side, with their chests cut open and pulled apart, primed for probing by the experts. He heard the screen door open and close, turned to see Howard, who held in his arms a live white hen with rust colored speckle. The way he carried the hen, not upside down, by the legs, but cradled in his arms, like a sick child, should have been a clue to the clueless nineteen year old, that a spritz of sensitivity might be in order. But, as Garth had once stipulated, in this business, there's little time for sentiment.

"Hey, Howard, how's it going?"

"Hi. I don't know what's wrong with her. She won't eat and can't walk too well, and seems like she can't see too well either, so I thought maybe you and the doctors could find out whats wrong, and maybe fix her up," he said as he held the semi-conscious bird out to Rhett.

Rhett thought he was kidding with the "fix her up" line. After forty years, he surely must have known that sick birds brought into the lab do not leave, alive, much less, cured.

"Sure, we'll fix her up, all right," Rhett replied as he took the bird from Howard, and, in a fleet motion, held its legs with one hand, broke its neck with the other, then tossed it, wings flailing, onto a pile of fresh corpses.

Howard was shocked, traumatized. He stiffened and froze, eyes wide in disbelief at the atrocity he'd witnessed. Mouth agape, he glared at Rhett, with his empty arms still outstretched. He then lowered his arms, slowly, not moving a now hateful hateful glare. Rhett was confused, "What? Is there a problem?"

Disgusted, Howard shook his head, turned and walked out, throwing the door open so violently, it slammed backwards against the wall that suspended it. Through the window, Rhett watched him walk away. He couldn't be sure, but it looked like Old Howard was sobbing.

That afternoon, on the drive home, as was always the routine, Snider and Rhett swapped stories about their day, with the FM on high.

"I think I got Old Howard mad at me," said Rhett, fishing for a little support.

"Why? What'd you do?"

"He brought in a sick bird."

"And?"

"And I killed it."

"Not in front of him, I hope."

"Well -- yeah. How else?"

"Oh, man, tell me you didn't do that."

"Why? I mean what the hell's the big deal here? I do this every day, ya know. The other guys don't look at me like I'm the anti Christ."

"You shouldn't have done that, Rhett. He loves those chickens. They're his family. His kids, even. He talks to 'em all day. Lee says that's why they out-lay all the other houses. Hell, he's even got names for most of 'em. You could've at least waited till he left."

"What you're saying is that I murdered one of his kids, right before his eyes."

"That about sums it up, Lucifer."

"Terrific."

So much for support. For the first time in his short life, that he was aware of, Rhett had hurt someone, deeply. It couldn't be trivialized by saying it's just some old guy who takes his chickens way too seriously. And even had that been the case, who was *he* hurting? No one. To whom was he a danger? No one, least of all, himself. Every living being has a right to happiness, and in Old Howard's eyes, that courtesy could certainly be extended to his chosen feathered family.

For the next few weeks, Rhett avoided situations that might lend themselves to the death duty, deferring to the more mundane tasks, such as rearranging supplies that didn't need rearranging, pulling weeds, or the ever present, always handy, manure duty. When there was no avoiding the inevitable lab tariff, he now waited for anyone who'd carried in a live sick bird, to be fully out of range, prior to the neck breaking ritual. Meanwhile, the end of Rhett's poultry tending vocation was clearly in sight.

During another such sunny afternoon, fraught with all the above procrastinations, as Rhett pulled weeds, on his knees, just outside the lab office, a station wagon ambled toward him on the dirt path, and skidded to a dusty stop, a few feet from him. Who should get out, but the blond girl from the front office, with a handful of mail. She walked, not to the door of the lab, to deliver the mail, but toward Rhett.

"Well, hi," she happily greeted, then continued, "just dropping off the mail. Weed duty, huh?"

He quipped, "Yeah, it's a tough job. Outside, fresh air, no bosses. But somebody's gotta do it."

They exchanged pleasantries, and Rhett got a closer look at the mystery girl. Up close, 'A.J.' as she called herself, was not nearly the appealing mystery goddess she'd been from a distance. Her aggressiveness only served to hasten the demise of his once flourishing, erotic pipe dream.

"You have such a friendly face," she said. Then, as she cleared a lock of hair from his forehead with her dainty finger, "and I love the way your hair hangs down in it, when you're working."

Rhett had to think of something, fast, to discourage, but not hurt her, and decided a crass reply, phrased politely, should do the trick.

"Well, thank you," he responded, "and I sure do like your perky little tits."

It didn't work. Her mouth dropped half open, but then smiled as though she'd just found the prize in her Wheaties. A.J. Glanced quickly down at her breasts and back up at Rhett.

"These old things? Thank you! I was actually hoping you'd notice. This blouse is kinda baggy. You could come over sometime when my parents aren't home and feel me under my clothes if you want. Oh, but that's all we can do because I'm a still a virgin, but, hey, tell you what, if you start going to our church and we talk to Pastor Fuzz about ---"

"Right, Pastor Fuzz. Look, that's a very kind offer, but I should tell you, I have a girlfriend and we're sorta, you know, engaged."

"Oh. Well, that's cool, it really is!" Then, as she offered her hand, "So, let's be friends, okay?"

"Sounds good to me."

With that, they shook hands. Hers was as clammy as Rhett's would have been, had he been on the receiving end of this emotional torpedo. 'Poor, sweet, desperate A.J.,' Rhett mused to himself, as she drove off, 'she'd taken us from complete strangers to the altar, in less than five minutes. If she had feathers, she could easily have been one of Howard's lost children. He'd have taken good care of her.'

Three or four days after the A.J. encounter, Snider drove himself and Rhett to work in his mother's minivan. For lunch, they got burgers from a nearby drive-in, and opted to lunch in the park that was provided exclusively for employees of the ranch. This was no ordinary park, with benches, pigeons or a manicured lawn. It qualified moreover as a five acre sampling of California's Big Basin or Avenue of the Giants. Huge Redwoods surrounded three small lakes, too big to classify as ponds. A narrow dirt road curled through the the trees on a hill, down and around the lakes. Endless hiking trails led throughout the park, and up the mountain, atop of which stood the owners' mansion.

Snider parked the van, facing the lowest lake, with the hill behind it. They sat quietly and watched the wooded serenity, while finishing the burger specials, after which Snider stretched out in the back of the van for a short nap. Rhett stayed in the front passenger seat, smoked a cigarette, and lost himself in speculation over where it's all going. *The job?* Garth had pulled him aside that morning and told him this job could pay off, big time, if he'd just stick with it. Rhett would give the matter some thought, but leaned more seriously toward an eventual amicable exit.

In the distance he could hear the faint sound of an engine, revving, that didn't register as more than a blended ambient sound of the country. The noise had no effect on Rhett's segueing daydreams, until he connected it, visually, to a car, A.J.'s station wagon. It hot-rodded down the hill, on the far side of the lake, way too fast for the narrow dirt road's conditions. The big clumsy wagon fish-tailed around every switchback turn, and left a plume of dust behind, that dramatically obscured the quiet, country landscape.

At the foot of the hill, A.J. throttled up as she got closer. When she tried to make a sharp turn that Snider and Rhett had bypassed on their way in, the wagon's front wheels turned right, but the car, on loose gravel, only half turned, skidded off the dirt road, and crashed, head-on, into one of the giant Redwoods. The lofty tree hadn't so much as quivered from the impact. Conversely, during the same half instant, the car was demolished.

Panicked, Rhett looked quickly back at Snider. The crash had been loud, but he slept through it.

"Snider!" Rhett yelled, as he wrenched the door open to get out, "Hey, go get help."

Snider propped himself up, groggily, on one elbow, "Huh? What?"

Assuming he could now see the wrecked car, Rhett directed, "Go get help, I'm gonna see if she's okay."

"What? What the hell are you talking about?"

"That!" he proclaimed, as he pointed at the carnage.

"Oh, shit."

"Just get some help."

Rhett grabbed a few leftover napkins from the burger bag, jumped out and trotted toward the wreck, while, behind him, the van sped off in the opposite direction.

The hood of the wrecked car was bowed upward from the impact.

It blocked Rhett's view of anything inside the car, thus, he knew not what to expect in the driver's seat, and braced for the worst.

A.J.'s face, hands and chest were covered with blood, from a deep gash that went the width of her chin. Aside from that, she appeared to be all right, as she sat, whimpering, behind the wheel, seatbelt still buckled. When Rhett approached, A.J. looked up at him and brought one hand to the gash on her chin, then held out both hands to him, in much the way Howard had, just after Rhett killed his friend.

"I feel so stupid," she said, amid the sobs, the tears and the blood.

"It's all right, A.J., accidents happen," he reassured her, "you're gonna be fine."

"No! Don't you get it? I was coming to see you -- I wanted to see *you*. Now this. I'm just such a stupid, ugly person. Oh, God, why couldn't I just die? It would've made things so much easier."

"Shhhh, now I know you don't mean any of that. Just take it easy and everything'll be fine. Try not to talk, okay?"

"Okay," she said quietly. Rhett gently pressed the napkins against her wound.

Shortly thereafter, Lee, the ranch foreman, drove up beside them, followed by Snider, in the van. Lee helped A.J. into his car, while she held the napkins to her chin. Rhett thought it peculiar that no ambulance was called, and that Lee would drive her to the hospital himself, battered and emotional as she'd been.

As Lee and the bloodied princess drove off, Snider called out to Rhett from the van, "You want a ride back to the lab?"

"No, thanks, I'll walk it"

He waved, departed, and Rhett was alone with the crumpled, forever silenced car. The serenity of the countryside had returned, now under a whole new set of circumstances.

Rhett drearily headed back to work, in no hurry to arrive. There were about 150 healthy birds, waiting for him to break their necks. Seems they'd all been injected with the wrong serum. He now believed he was no better than Hitler, who'd had no more regard for human life than Rhett had for the lives of these vertebrates. Never mind that they were just chickens. They had eyes, hearts, brains, such as they were, and their needs for happiness were simple. But, even as simple as those needs were, they'd not be allowed to pursue them. One entity, higher up on the food chain, decided, in the wink of an eye, that they were expendable. When he got back to the lab, Rhett gave a week's notice.

Phase I

At an informal gathering, the rebel was unexpectedly found by the truest love of his life. She touched his lips and awakened him with an instant warmth that shot from his flushed face to the soles of his feet. A warmth and completeness not felt since he slumbered restlessly in the darkness of the womb, with a craving that, by itself, ignited a lurking, perpetual insanity. Her sweet and subtle force may kill him, over time, if not from her influence, then just from her effect, but his faithfulness shall never waiver. He'll give for her his life and expect nothing more than her soothings in return. She'll give him courage. In time, after his dependance is affirmed and reaffirmed, she'll steady his limbs. She'll never say no. She'll never disappoint. She'll always be there for his comfort only. He trusts in her from this night forward. He'll forsake anything and anyone to preserve their union, just to be with her, to wallow in her false praise and empty reassurances, temporary as they remain. She'll cost money, but only in small amounts. She'll cost freedoms, but they're over rated. She'll cost memories, but only until she returns. While others are casual and responsible with her presence, he will embrace her and her alone for all her magical powers that only he is privileged to know. She's too long awaited, his newfound drug of choice, and they've not yet even cemented their vows. Tonight her cork was crystallized, tho had ne'er an effect on the Mountain Rhine sweetness of her fruits. Could it be she's waited just as long for him? For now, their bond of till death us do part is nobody's business but hers. And everyone he'll hurt.

Truth in Advertising

Desperate for work, you've responded to an ad in the Help Wanted section of the classifieds. If your interviewer, a twenty something dweeb, with George McFly hair, tells the *tru*th about your first foray into the drive-thru-life trade, it could sound something like this:

"You can make five hundred dollars a week at this job. It's easy, no stress. Just do it and make money."

"Uh huh."

"We'll load you into a van with eleven other drivers, mostly illiterate single mothers, deadbeat dads and paroled child molesters. One of the women is a suicidal manic depressive, one of the men is a drug dealer, and they all bathe after every UFO sighting. But, hey, they have drivers licenses, and that's all we care about."

"Uh huh."

"First, the driver of the van, probably the suicide, who aspires to die in a horrendous car crash, by the way, will hand you a slip of paper with the make, model and VIN number of the car you'll be delivering. She'll then drive all of you to an auto auction yard, where you'll see more cars in one place than you've ever seen in your life. Row after row after endless row of parked cars.

"You'll be let out of the van, then your job will be to find the car that matches the one described on your slip of paper, and drive it out of the yard, to whichever used car dealer has purchased it. That dealer's car lot could be a short drive across town. Or it could be seventy miles down the freeway."

"Uh huh."

"But we're getting ahead of ourselves. Let's go back to when you've finally found your one-in-4,000 car. The first thing you're going to want to do is check the fluid levels. Water, oil, transmission. No, wait, before you do that, make sure the car starts. This way, if it does start, you'll get an inaccurate oil level reading when you check it. So, if there's only a thimble full of oil in it, and you blow a rod on the freeway, our company won't be responsible. You will. But don't despair, we'll pay the damages and withhold half your paycheck until you've paid us back.

"This may all be moot, since the battery in your car will probably be dead, because the car has no doubt been parked on the lot since the Reagan administration. If the battery *is* dead, wait about forty five minutes for the lot attendant -- he's the one with open facial lesions and green teeth, driving a golf cart -- to come and give you a jump.

"Next, you'll have to check the car's body for dents and scratches. Please notate every little dent, ding or scratch on the slip of paper given you by Ms. Manic. If you miss a dent and the dealer finds it, you'll have to pay for that too, but remember our handy installment plan. Still with me?"

"Uh huh."

"Good. Now, remember also to bring cash in case the car is out of gas, and chances are, it will be. Don't worry, we'll reimburse you. Well, unless, of course, you owe us money."

"Uh huh."

"Okay, let's review. You've found the car, checked the fluid levels, inspected it for dents, gotten a jump-start, put gas in it and now you're on the road. The obvious next step is the safe delivery of the car, right?"

"Uh huh."

"When you arrive at your destination, you'll have to find someone to sign for the car. This could be a sticking point, since no one will want to be responsible for accepting the wreck you just sputtered in with. Again, don't despair. If you continually badger the sales force, like a beggar with a tin cup, eventually, someone will sign for it, just to get you out of their hair. Capiche?

"Uh huh."

"I'll be right back with some papers for you to sign."

Sales Pitch

Your next questionable classified: A rewarding career in magazine subscription sales.

Today must be your lucky day
And you'll sure get a lift
When I offer you these
Magazine subscriptions as a gift!

There is the little matter
Of the postage handling charge-
It's only thirty cents a week
Now, that won't be so hard.

We'll double it, then triple it
To get those payments down
Find a helpful figure
That's doable and round.

The cents turn into dollars
And the dollars due delight
'cause you now owe us fifty a week
For the rest of your natural Life.

The Class of '68

As a child, when I'd hear the phrase 'gas war,' my mind conjured images of gas station attendants, armed with pump nozzles, who'd take aim at each other from behind barricades or the safety of their respective trenches. But then, I also thought the North Korean Guerrillas, so often referred to in nightly newscasts, were *real* gorillas, with guns, and you probably shouldn't make them mad. As a seventeen year old, employed at the local independent gas & mini-mart, I came to know gas wars as a bonanza, when the sole winner was the consumer, paying as little as nineteen cents for a gallon of regular. That was one of four jobs, held consecutively, by your intrepid narrator, in the year, summed up by American historians as "one goddamn thing after another," 1968.

I'd always tried to make a habit of asking at least one stupid question to christen each new employment experience, and always on the first day of work. Hank's Royal Gas and Mini-Mart was no exception. I'd grown up watching pump jockeys wash windshields and check oil, and thought, in some perverse way, this appeared to be a pretty cool career choice. Never mind that they made very little money, were always filthy, and never smiled. It was all part of the allure.

I smiled for my first customer and, after he ordered five dollars' worth, asked him, "Check that water and oil for ya?"

He chuckled, "Yeah, be sure and check that water."

So, what's so funny about checking the water in a Volkswagen?

"I, uh – meant the battery water."

"Sure you did, kid. Nice save."

Though I continued to do business there for a number of years, the job only lasted a few months, until the minimum wage made an insurmountable leap from $1.40 to $1.60 an hour, and half the staff was laid off.

Home Town High School had a work experience program that included half-days at school. I made immediate use of it. One of the perks of the program was a job referral list. My first referral, after the massive gas station lay-off, was to Premiere Office Supply and Business Machines. They needed an after school delivery driver. As they'd only recently opened their doors, I'd be the first of what would surely be many.

The business owner, a Dick York look-alike and sound-alike, was a nice enough, hard working guy; his wife, friendly, helpful, cheerful and drop dead gorgeous. She surely was much more of a help than a hindrance in landing those big accounts, to which I'd soon deliver paper and typewriter ribbons. She was no Liz Montgomery, though every bit as bewitching.

On Tuesdays only, instead of the company van, I drove the

wife's more compact Ford Falcon. I grew to love Tuesdays. She'd help me load the packages into the back seat of the Falcon. Her attire was never business-like, but generally tight and bright. V-neck sweaters and mini skirts, almost always fire engine red. She'd load the deliveries from one side of the car, while I, the tenderfoot sex addict, loaded from the other, hoping not to get caught, peering down into the ever present cleavage of a goddess.

It was on one of those Tuesdays that my tenure as the premiere delivery boy would come to a crashing halt. Literally. Dick -- might as well call him that -- had reminded me more than once to always use the seat belts. They were still a fairly novel safety concept, not yet standard on most new cars, so he apparently thought I needed the reminders. Fact is, I liked using them, thus needed no prompting. But, on those shorter trips, with only a block or two between stops, and never a top speed limit over thirty five, what could possibly happen that would require a seat belt? Dubious logic in tow, I'd remain beltless for the abbreviated jaunts.

The force of the broadside hit from the Chevy wagon threw me to the passenger side of the car. I momentarily blacked out, awakened by the slide guitar lead-in to Henson Cargill's "Skip a Rope" on the radio. It was the only machine left functional after the crash. The first thing I saw, amid the shattered safety glass on the floorboard, were all the push-pull knobs from the underside of the dash, that had been sheared off by the force of the impact. I must've been in shock, as I was in no hurry to exit the totaled car. I did take a quick inventory of my own person. No blood, no aches or pains, and all the important stuff -- arms, legs, neck -- still worked. One small scratch on the left palm was all I could find. During my quick perusal of the damage, I couldn't help noticing the door on the driver's side, where I'd sat prior to the crash. It was caved inward to a perfect point, right about where my ribs had been. Later, in a more conscious state, I realized that a seat belt would've held me in place, and probably shattered the left side of my rib cage, punctured a lung or maybe a heart valve or two. For the record, I still use seat belts and shoulder harnesses, especially on short distance jaunts.

The tow truck driver gave me a ride back to the office, after dropping off the finished Falcon, undelivered packages still intact, at a local wrecking yard. The boss's lovely wife was watching the store, alone. I was certain that by now she knew what had happened, though, oddly, she didn't.

We sat down and I broke the news about her demolished car. She took it well. All she wanted to know was if she could get the packages out of the car, a question I couldn't answer. Otherwise, she was glad I was all right, and seemed unconcerned about the condition of her car. Strange how, not even an hour before, I should have a near-death experience, but as we talked, my seventeen year old thought processes, held hostage by an out of control, post pubescent libido, would focus only on what style of panties she might be wearing. French cut? Bikini? Surely not granny-style. Let's stay focused on the issue at hand: I could've been killed! True enough, but I wasn't. Gotta be bikini style, with a nicely embroidered *Tuesday*.

Dick called me at home that evening, sympathetic and glad I was okay, but added the oddly phrased question, "Well, do you think you should come back to work?"

I guessed he wanted to hear me beg for my job, and promise to be more careful in the future. But I merely returned his cordiality, answering his question in the negative, something he seemed relieved to hear. It was a relief for me, too, though I couldn't help inwardly lamenting, no more tight sweaters, no more pantie fantasies or possible, but realistically improbable quickies in the store room. Maybe I should have gone ahead and begged.

I was one of those who turned eighteen during his last school year, while others would have to wait till after they graduated to be old enough to smoke and register for the draft. The '57 Plymouth I bought from Dad had become a '60 Chevy, purchased at a used car lot. I made a new circle of friends, most of whose limited politics were conservative, and each of whom smoked a lot of weed, but did not work or drive.

To follow the delivery boy collapse, I gained employment at the local motor hotel, where I bussed tables in the dining room and ran out the occasional room service order, which qualified me, in the eyes of the union, as a waiter.

On this hot June night, it seems all is well. Work's been gainful. Mary, an older, career server in the dining room, hands me ten dollars, on my way out, declaring she's just "sharing the wealth," after receiving a humongous tip from a party of five. We get along capitally, do Mary and I. She has a daughter, my age, whom I've known since age twelve, and with whom I danced, cheek-to-cheek, at an after-school garage party in 1962. When I think about that day, so fondly etched into my memory, I swear I can smell hair spray and bubblegum.

At 11:02pm I punch a time card in the kitchen, wave to the chef on my way out. He's happy, waves back, must be a Democrat. He keeps an eye on his portable black & white TV, and maintains his grin, as he scrapes the grill clean.

At 11:05pm I start the Chevy, back out of a space, worm through and out of the motor hotel parking lot. The trip home will be short, a little over a mile. I leave the radio off.

At 11:08pm I make a turn, up the long grade that leads home. The street is quiet, maybe too quiet, even for this late hour, in our semi-rural community.

At 11:12pm I make a left turn into the gravelly horseshoe driveway that encircles our house. As always, Dad has left the back porch light on for me.

At 11:13pm Ferrel cats scatter in all directions, as I walk from the car to the back door of the house. I open it and step into the dark passage that gives way to the near-dark of the kitchen, lit dimly by a television screen, one room away. Confusion and chaos emanates from that TV.

At 11:15pm Bobby Kennedy is en route to his death bed.

The following morning, just a few hours after RFK breathed his last, Home Town High School's class of '68 staged the school's second ever sit-in/class boycott, which took place on the senior patio. The first had been for Martin Luther King, the morning after his assassination, just two months earlier. I attended both. It was only June. What the hell else could possibly happen in this crazy year?

Another event I'd attended, but told no one in my small circle of apolitical friends about, was an anti-war rally, on and around the steps of the Oakland Induction Center. I knew little about the Viet Nam war, and, determined to find some logic and common sense to attach to how it all began, set out to get all sides of the story. Without going into a lot of boring detail surrounding my dogged investigation, I can honestly report that war, in any form, is totally devoid of logic or common sense. It starts and is perpetuated by irrational people with way too much power.

Since a passing grade in American History was a requirement for graduation, and since I'd failed said course, as a junior, it was necessary for me to repeat it, as a senior. But the second go-round would be taught by an instructor with a flare for realism. She'd forced us to take a hard look at *all* the American wars, from the one out of which our nation was born, to the one now known as a police action, because it's never been legally declared. Regardless of the label, people on both sides had died, and continue to die, violently, in droves. Soon, the instructor pointed out, it'd be my turn to take a step forward and swear to kill the enemy, a prospect more appealing to some than others. And it was at her insistence that before passing judgement on the thousands of young people who'd taken to the streets in protest, from Columbia University to Berkeley, perhaps it'd be wise to give them a listen. So, off I went to Oakland. My first truly patriotic act.

Back at the senior patio RFK memorial, I saw many familiar faces, some of whom would quip to their neighbor and laugh out loud, at what, I don't know. But this was a somber event. A wake. Hardly the place for child-like snickers. They'd done the same thing for Rabbit's graveside service, two years prior. Hundreds of students who'd never even met him, saw an opportunity to cut class, and when asked by the dean, the day after the service, why they hadn't come to school after the service, would falsely lament that he'd been their "best friend." How enlightened the dean surely must have been to learn that this student's memorial was attended by no less than 300 of his closest friends.

Once upon a time, I really had been Rabbit's best friend, but his other best friends, all 300 of them, had made it impossible for me to tell the truth. Since he (the dean) saw through their phoniness, he ordered them, one by one, to bring another note from home. When eventually, it came my turn to answer for my absence, I was forced to lie, saying I was tired, and simply went straight home after the service. He sent me on to class.

I swore someday I'd expose those middle class, adolescent frauds, who'd exploited the deaths of my friend and RFK, in the interest of widening their comfort zones. And now I have. I feel much better, thank you.

Dad wanted me to be an electrician. Mom wanted me to join the Air Force. My mother wanted me to do something, anything creative. The Army just wanted me. The artistic option was the most attractive, and the one with the strongest pull, but my chosen art form would have to wait at least until the car was paid off.

Most fathers want their sons to grow up in their image. Even though Dad was technically a step-grandfather, he was the only father I'd ever known, and I, his only son. Hence, his wish for me to make the same career choice. After graduation, he arranged with the Union for me to be hired with the official job title of 'helper.' *His* helper, at a rate of $3.50 an hour. That kind of money in 1968, for anyone my age, was comparable to the Mother Lode.

As jobs go, this one had nothing in the way of exciting, humorous or even interesting anecdotes. It was simply eight hours of hard work, pulling wire, sidestepping carpenters and sheetrockers, and counting the minutes to the next union sanctioned break. I didn't have much in common with the other construction types, except the younger house painters, who had longer hair, and who Dad surmised were more than likely only in it for the fumes.

These were sprawling, subdivided tracts of new homes, all with essentially the same floor plan, thus it wasn't hard to memorize the drill. Just pull the wire, strip the ends, nail up the boxes, four studs in from the door, and move on to the next duplicate structure. We were one small, but necessary phase of Pete Seeger's ticky-tacky that would eventually reaffirm the overall message of his timeless Little Boxes song.

"People gotta live somewhere," Dad would say, then add, "but you wouldn't catch me living in one of these cracker boxes."

He'd been careful not to berate the concept too zealously, as it had, after all, provided steady work for him, and now for me.

That wasn't the first time I'd been known, personally or professionally, as Dad's helper. As a small child, past the diaper stage, but still too young to pull wire, he'd take me with him to an occasional Saturday side job, done without the knowledge of the union, for under-the-table cash. If anyone asked about me, or said "Hi" to me, his stock response, with a humorous slant remained, "Yeah, I had to bring my helper with me."

One such side job wasn't for cash, but for a dog. A purebred, papered Irish Terrier. A full day's work wouldn't quite cover the cost of a healthy puppy, however, the breeder just happened to have a ten month old male that had broken its leg during a cat chase. Though the leg was now healed, it disqualified the dog from any showing, thus it could be had at a cut rate, for breeding purposes, which was Dad's plan. He'd put it immediately out to stud.

We named the dog Laddy. He wasted no time becoming a beloved family member and potential money maker. Just one flaw in the master plan: Laddy shot blanks. On three occasions, before it became obvious, they'd sequester the sire with a purebred bitch in heat, in the back porch. The door was windowed, thus, the arguably happy couple could be monitored for actual physical contact. He'd give the bitch an occasional token hump, scarcely enough to qualify as mating. But his mind, it seemed, was unquestionably not on his job.

It wouldn't be fair to say Laddy was totally asexual. He actually had an above average carnal appetite. Just not for dogs. On any given afternoon, he could be found in the back yard, having his way with one of ten or twelve feral cats. They were wild, never to be touched by human hands, but, oddly, welcomed Laddy's advances, staying submissively still for the slow, methodical procedure. His preference was the Manx variety, perhaps because they had no tail to obscure a direct entry.

Dad never had much luck in the small business game, though not for lack of honesty, trust and hard work. It was always the honesty and trust that got him into trouble. His short lived electrical contracting business of the late 1940s, staffed exclusively by prison parolees, might have been a success, save for the unpaid accounts and parolees' sticky fingers. Add to that, an entire Saturday, plus cash outlay, in return for a purebred dog that only humps cats.

Somebody's Baby

Somewhere, sometime, somebody's baby is born
In the same somewhere, the same sometime, a family rejoices
Pictures are shared, compliments paid,
Announcements are sent, parents beam pride

In the same sometime, while a different somewhere
Somebody's baby has grown to a man,
Whose wealth and power deigns
hardship for many, happiness for but a few in the king's circle

With a flick of his wrist or the grace of his pen,
Somebody's baby can and will poison
Thousands, to satisfy the boundless cravings of
His power, his wealth, his kingdom

Decades later, in a war of his doing,
Somebody's baby never lends a thought to
Somebody's baby, who's taken a bullet, that
Causes somebody's mother to weep.

Bleu Gene Caper

"I have two hundred dollars in travelers checks. I'll give you a hundred and eighty of it to take me back to California right now."

Such was the impassioned request of Carson Bleu, to the driver sent to collect him at Washington National Airport, following his first few gulps of the hot, liquefied, East Coast aura that qualifies as air in August.

The driver, an earthy, good natured blond woman named Mona, chuckled at the thought. "This is about the humidity, right?" she asked as they exited the parking lot in a rented U-Haul van, "You'll get used to it. Everybody else does. Just plan on taking lots of showers. What you may not get used to is the traffic. Not much road courtesy here."

"Doesn't look any worse than San Francisco."

"It's Sunday night. Wait till the morning commute," she countered, "you'll earn your stripes."

While the following day's morning commute was everything promised, for Carson, it was tolerable. And it better be, since driving was ostensibly the sole reason for his trip, from the West Coast to the East. He was here to be a driver, as he'd been in California, for a disabled adult. Patsy, the recipient of Carson's driving skills, had landed a job in the Capitol Hill office of a New Jersey senator. Along with other less meaningful trips, it would be Carson's job to get her safely tucked into the Senator's chambers, Monday through Friday.

The first journey went without a hitch, with only one back seat driving effort from Patsy, reminding Carson to "Make a left at the corner, and watch out for that truck. The driver looks mean."

"Just get out and beat him up, Patsy."

"We don't have time," she replied, as though his suggestion had been in earnest.

To follow the drop-off, Carson had some time on his hands. A little under eight hours. He'd need other part time work to fill the void, thus, his sight seeing tour would double as a casual job hunt.

Evening found Carson responding, by way of a cross town bus, to a classified ad for a roommate on Capitol Hill. With Patsy back in her apartment, the van stayed in the garage, and his own transportation would become annoyingly public. The bus ride was squeaky and bumpy, though he was thankful for the protection, as he stared out at the Northeast Washington ghetto. The streets could have been a third world playground for children who, well after dark, should have been at home, and who paid no mind to the rabbit sized rats that occasionally ambled across the street, and into the nearest storm drain.

It was a townhouse. One in a row of many, with wrought iron stairs and railings. Carson was greeted by an early twenties woman,

Amy, who offered him ice water, as she sat on the kitchen floor, reweaving the seat of an antiquated wooden dinette chair. Her dark brown, frizzy hair was tied back; a hatchet chinned smile was ever present, throughout the interview.

He said all the right things. California native; new in town; three years at last address; working as driver for the disabled. The 'California' part scored extra points. Apparently, to a lifetime east coast resident, the streets really are paved with gold in Carson's native state, and who was he to invalidate the myth?

His room would be the living room. A small, single, frameless bed, now adorned with bedspread and throw pillows, would be where he'd sleep. The remainder of the time, the room would be used in the usual communal manner, and the bed, as a communal couch, as there were two other house mates, not present for the interview.

"Oh, and we do have central air conditioning," Amy interjected, then added, "but we never use it."

"Why not?"

"It costs too much to run. Besides, I prefer natural to artificial air. Don't you?"

"To a degree," Carson responded, "That degree being about seventy five."

Carson's work schedule filled up over the next few months. There did, however, remain those idle, unfilled hours from 6pm to midnight. The house mates were all in bed by ten, around the hour our west coast transplant sprang to life.

The need for cooler, dryer air drew Carson like a magnet to every saloon within a mile of the abode where his welcome was being rapidly worn out. The fact that he drank all their beer and cranked up the AC while the three house mates were at work, hadn't endeared Carson much to them. He'd eventually replace the beer and make good for the difference in the utility bill, but the damage was done.

The turn that would ultimately seal Carson's fate in Amy's perfect household, and send him packing, about a week after its culmination, was a late night tryst between himself and Amy. Seems he'd staggered in from another evening of alcoholic frivolity, and found her, in an equally drunken state, masturbating on his bed.

"Oops. I guess I'm caught," she casually confessed, as the busier hand, beneath her unzipped jeans, froze in place, "I'll leave if you want."

They did say it was a communal couch. With that in mind, Carson decided she had a right.

"No, I think you should probably finish what you started."

Sex changes all relationships, and this would be no exception.

Patsy and Carson parted ways, amicably, after he found a room to rent, and no longer needed to live out of the van, the result of Amy's swift kick. Although she never said as much, Carson believed Patsy was concerned for her safety, with him at the wheel. And who could blame her? What with his having drawn fewer and fewer sober breaths, while becoming more acclimated to the D.C. lounge circuit.

In one of those cool, dry saloons, Mr. Harvey's, a rumored gay

Capitol Hill hangout, Carson found a turkey sandwich to fit perfectly within the boundaries his budget: Free. No, not purchased for him by a hopeful gay pick-up, but actually on the house, served with a sexy smile and all the right garnishes, by a beautiful red haired siren with an endearing southern accent, and a plan.

A few miles on Pennsylvania Avenue can be the difference between world history and a small sausage pizza. On one block of the storied thoroughfare, a disgraced President made his farewell speech, while on another, at precisely the same moment, Carson completed an application to become a waiter in a basement eatery called Rivington's. He used and embellished culinary experience from six to eight years earlier, to bolster his chances, though once again, the California roots, alone, prevailed as an asset. Henceforth, he was in.

On New Years Day, Carson sat and nurses the traditional mother of all hangovers, on the bottom step of a staircase that led from the street, down into the humble burger and pizza hangout. For the more pretentious and well-dressed, there was the street level restaurant of the same name, with its more dignified, bib and lobster fare.

Save for the bartender, Patrick, Carson had been the only server scheduled. The duly licensed management, so expertly trained in the habits of restaurant clientèle, had predicted next to no business for this holiday, and even considered not opening at all. To lure in the presumed smattering of sidewalk traffic, the experts had advertised a New Year's Day special on the small chalkboard, just outside the front door. Steak and Eggs, $2.99!

The first party, a party of four, meandered in, a half hour after opening. As Carson advised them to "Go ahead and sit anywhere," he began to think maybe the experts were right. This could be the only business he does all day. Lucky him. He'd put in his time, return home to the warmth of his rented room, and go back to bed.

Better put a hold on that back-to-bed scenario. As he took this party's order for steak and eggs all around, complimented by a round of Bloody Marys, Carson couldn't help but notice, over his shoulder, the steady filing in of a throng, anxious to enjoy the day's special. Had a tour bus stopped at their door? By the time he finished writing the first order, every table in the house was full. Those who couldn't find an open table were seated at the bar. Bloody Marys, gin fizzes, eight ounce sirloins and eggs for everybody.

With a handful of guest checks, all filled out and ready to hang, Carson flew up the two flights of utility stairs, into the kitchen, where four short order cooks, with time to kill, were huddled at one end of the prep line, engaged in a bullshit session.

As Carson thumbed through the guest checks, he called out the orders, "Steak and eggs, rare and O.E.; steak and eggs, medium and scrambled; steak and eggs, medium rare and sunny up; steak and eggs, well and over easy; three steak and eggs, all rare, with scrambled; two steak and eggs, both medium, with over easy; five steak and eggs, all medium well, two scrambled, three O.E.--"

But no one was cooking. They all just chuckled, until he began to hang the orders. Then, one of them got it, "Hey, he's not kidding," and the bullshit session reluctantly broke up.

As Carson headed back down the stairs, Eli, the line chef, called after him, "Better start your toast!"

"Toast? They get toast?"

It is at this moment our harried server launches a new breakfast tradition. No toast.

"I don't have time," Shouted Carson, back to Eli, from halfway down the first flight of stairs, "We'll let 'em have more potatoes. What the hell do they want for three bucks?"

Back downstairs, the bar was almost full, and a line was forming that backed up the front stairs. Meanwhile, Carson hadn't even taken half of the orders for those who were seated at tables. As he rang up the drink orders at the service bar, he made an emergency request to Patrick, who was busy with a half built row of Bloody Marys, "When you get a minute, can you call upstairs, and get a host down here to help out?"

"I'll see what I can do," he responded, then added, "but you'll get richer if you work it alone."

An hour later, most of the steaks had been sent back. Carson had been up and down those utility stairs like a yo yo. "This one's too well done, this one's too rare, this one's not rare enough, this one's not medium enough, oh, and this one's too well done, with eggs over easy, not scrambled," and so on.

Finally, predictably, as Carson placed another return in the pick-up window from whence it came, Eli informed him, "I ain't touchin' one more goddamn steak."

"Would a little Mississippi Mud help you touch it, Eli?"

"You bet your white ass it would, and it better be on your tray, next trip up, or you're gonna be back here, cookin' this shit yourself. In fact, make it a whole damn round. It's gettin' too hot for all of us back here."

"Blackmail doesn't become you, Eli."

On Carson's next sweat soaked visit to the service bar, prior to running up ten more breakfast orders, "Gimme four Muds for the kitchen, on me."

As Patrick built four tall cool ones, he advised, "You're gonna spoil those guys."

"Maybe, but it beats cooking all those breakfasts myself."

Two hours later, the rush had subsided. Carson pulled the 'specials' sign when they ran out of steaks. He'd single handedly sold the last 200 of them. The host from upstairs never showed, but, now $300 richer, Carson's Mississippi real estate investment had paid off nicely. And not one of them ever got toast.

The red haired southern girl with a free turkey sandwich and a plan -- we'll call her Jet – wasted no time getting familiar with the kid from California. On that first day they met, as she glided around the one-room bar and restaurant, delivering lunch specials, she fielded a bevy of bad jokes from the regulars, about her new blue jeans, which were hard to miss. They fit her, tightly, like a motorman's glove, accentuating a posterior that even the gayest of men, seated at the bar, could appreciate, as one of nature's finer achievements.

Each time she passed Carson's table or stopped to perform an unnecessary task, such as shining the ash tray with a bar napkin, Jet had another question. Live close by? Where you from? Ever going back? Where do you work? Married? Girlfriend? All the questions that, amid the heterosexual mating game, are generally reserved for the masculine end.

Conversely, Carson had only one question for her. It was the equally direct and typically male. "What time do you get off?"

Later that afternoon, like the dedicated Pavlovian dog, Carson returned to Mr. Harvey's, where he and Jet got cozy over Irish Coffees. She'd changed into a t-shirt and coveralls, and was just as talkative as she'd tried to be, between the service of those pesky customers. While he'd never been one to over analyze the proverbial gift horse, especially when it's in the form of a fair skinned redhead, throwing herself at him, Carson couldn't help but notice this situation getting curiouser and curiouser.

"You seem to be on pretty good terms with the bartender," he said, after having also noticed her earlier constant good natured pawing of said bartender, and occasionally pulling him aside, for what appeared to be intensely personal conversations. He was an otherwise jovial sort. Tall, thin, balding on top, with a pony tail that reached the base of his spine.

"Yeah, that's Bert, the guy I live with -- oh, but we ain't lovers. We broke up, and we're just room mates now. Hell, we don't even sleep in the same bedroom anymore. He's sleeping on the couch till he finds another place and moves out. We're still good friends, though. When did you say you're goin' back to California?"

"A couple months, I guess. As soon as I save enough money."

Further on into the marathon verbal foreplay, among other intimate details of their relationship, Jet let slip that Bert, like your author's childhood pet, had no lead in his pencil, or, in her words, "Can't have no kids. He's sterile as a doctor's knife. But don't tell him I told you that. He's kinda sensitive about it."

They didn't have to order any rounds. The parade of spiked coffee drinks, each one stronger than the last, was relentless, all compliments of Bert and their waiter, Ricky Ricardo. More about him, later. Finally, Carson decided, while still ambulatory, it was time for some fresh air. As much fresh air as they could take, on a stroll back to his room, a few blocks away, ostensibly for a look at the late night movie on channel twelve. When they stood up to leave, and said their goodbyes to the lounge crowd, even given his advanced inebriated state, Carson had an uneasy feeling about what surely must've been on Bert's mind. He'd watched his alleged former girlfriend leave with someone she'd literally picked up, maybe eight hours earlier. Not sure he could handle that, had Carson been in Bert's sandals.

Back at the rooming house, while none too quietly, Carson and Jet managed to fumble through his keys and find their way inside the dark, quiet hallway. His room was three doors in, on the right. As he found another correct key to unlock the door, Jet whisked past him, into the room, after which he turned to close the door and bring up the lights.

Meanwhile, as she walked toward the bed, her back to Carson, Jet imparted, "You'll have to excuse me, but when I want something,

I don't like to waste a bunch of time with any of that silly foreplay or word game shit."

By the last word of the above true confession, Jet was nude. Breakaway coveralls? So goes the anomaly that women can wear twice as many clothes as men, and be out of them in half the time.

A few hours later, the worn out couple lay on their backs and shared an after-play smoke. As she stared up at the ceiling, Jet noted, "Wow, you diddled me three, four -- five times, and the sun ain't even up yet."

"Yeah. Must be the Irish Coffee."

During the weeks that followed, Bert and Carson had, somewhat ironically, become good friends. The three of them engaged in many a recreational activity that usually involved music, food or movies. They were often accompanied by Ricky Ricardo, the fourth wheel, so nicknamed, not for the sitcom legend, but for a line in the Jimmy Buffet song, "Pencil Thin Mustache." He wasn't Spanish or Cuban. Originally from Texas, with an accent that nearly matched Jet's, he was as fair skinned as the other three, with only a roundness and receding blond hairline that set him apart. He could've been the model for the Pillsbury Dough Boy, though it should be noted, his vocabulary and perceptive ability rivaled Carson's stereotypical image of anyone from a state in which everything is measured by the shitload.

During their more private moments, Carson and Jet hatched a plan that saw her accompanying him back to California, and the two of them living together, probably in Oakland. However, getting a candid view of the everyday Jet, Carson's misgivings about traveling anywhere with her, let alone, coast to coast in a Volkswagen, mounted more by the hour. She had a temper to match her hair color, and a long winded opinion, usually baseless, about everything. The endearing Southern drawl, for Carson, had become a dreaded monotone. At some point, he wondered if this was all a show for his benefit. And, if so, why? Bert was a patient, even tempered person, with a good sense of humor, but Carson couldn't imagine even him, living day to day, with an intemperate volcano on two legs. These numbers simply didn't add up.

A few days prior to their scheduled departure, Carson arranged to share a ride and expenses with someone who was driving to Denver. From there, He'd catch a Greyhound, home. Why didn't he tell Jet? Because he knew she'd cancel, even with only days to go.

On Carson's last day at Rivington's, just before the lunch rush, as anticipated, Jet wandered in for a "Little talk." He sat her in a booth and gave her coffee, then sat opposite her for the full effect of her, laying down one final law. That's how she'd always spoken, like a strict mother, laying down the law.

"The trip's off. I couldn't live with you. You're too jealous," she announced, in obvious anticipation of a dish rattling defense.

But a mild mannered correction was what Jet got. Carson calmly explained, "First of all, the trip's not off. I'm leaving, on schedule, tomorrow, with a ride-share I arranged. Second, if the jealousy you're claiming has anything to do with that morning, at four o'clock, when you got out of bed and spent the next two hours with Bert, on the couch in the living room, hell, honey, anybody'd be a little curious.

I'm sorry if you thought my asking where you've been all that time constituted jealousy."

"Well, you drink too much, anyway, and I can't be around a guy -- wait, you made other plans? Without telling me?"

"Uh huh."

"We were supposed to leave tomorrow, you know. What if I got the car all packed and ready to go?"

"I knew you wouldn't."

At that, she stood up and solemnly offered her hand to shake, "Well, it's been nice knowing you."

As Carson accepted the handshake, "Goodbye, Jet. Best to Bert."

Years later, Carson sped along a narrow stretch of lonely Central Valley highway. Like Frank, a horse that once pulled his handsome cab in Georgetown, and who'd break into a full gallop when he could smell the comfort of his stable close by, Carson caught himself pushing a little harder on the accelerator, in anticipation of the comforts of home. Remembering Frank brought a smirk and a momentary reexamination of that chapter in his youth. A question still remained. Had he been a made-to-order sperm donor, in a well crafted plan to give Jet the baby that Bert couldn't? Perhaps had he not been so perpetually drunk, he'd have noticed a lot more than just the *little* signs that piqued his curiosity. Perhaps with a clearer mind, he'd have known in an instant, that he was about to father a child he'd never see.

With a slight strain of his imaginative assets, Carson could see a translucent image of Frank, at a full, majestic gallop, beside his car. Just before he eclipsed Carson's eighty miles per hour, Frank glanced briefly over at him, to be sure he'd follow his lead. Go, Frank, go. You're almost home.

A Procrastinator's Plea

Let the dentist's chair lean back
for anyone but me
till I can't stand the pain another tick.
Let the leaky faucet go
another bucket full or so,
or until I find a wrench I think will fit.

Let the Christmas shopping wait
till the stores are open late
or until about an hour before they close.
Let the parking ticket fine,
for which I'll need to stand in line,
stay inside its complimentary envelope.

Let my taxes and their forms
keep the other late things warm,
while I conjure clever ways to put them off.
Let the card receipts and stats
multiply like little rats,
and bless my other more delinquent stuff.

Let all those jobs that aren't much fun
go unfinished or undone
as the interest and the penalties accrue.
I'll get to them with haste
when there's no more time to waste
And I've absolutely nothing else to do.

Phase II

The rebel sleeps alone in the dimly lit confines of a petite wooden shanty. Its floors are caked with sticky filth, dust blankets the windows, nicotine and rancid garbage permeate the atmosphere. During the months that led up to now, he's forsaken all who would stand in the way of his union with the truest love of his life, meanwhile avoiding eye contact with his reflection in any mirror. By now, he's witnessed, even befriended hundreds of others who'd fallen helplessly under her spell, then yielded to her grasp. She does not discriminate. She'll take anyone, from any ethnicity, social circle or income level. The rebel proudly held that they were all weak, possessed not of his independent will. Meanwhile, She's continued to steady his limbs, she's never said no, never disappointed, always been there for his comfort only, and all at the mere expense of his livelihood, his withered sanity, his freedoms, his family, and soon, his home. They're all no match for her magical powers. This maverick, who once enjoyed a procession of options that stretched from ground to cosmos, now awakens on the floor, curled up beside empty bottles, in a corner of the shanty. All but two of the options have steadily diminished. He can use what remains of his rebellious might to wrest control of his life away from her. Or he can trust in her magical powers one last time, and hazard certain death.

Pictures to Burn

When last we left Jonathon, our bartender and childhood victim of religious buffoonery, he was awakening in his car, from a reality inspired dream. Now, years later, we find him on the cusp of the great American career change. As he stood behind the bar, in a sparsely occupied Sunday night lounge, Jonny scripted a carefully worded, polite letter of resignation, on half a sheet of binder paper. But he was a bit uneasy about his impending leap from part time barman, to full time white collar professional. He'd joked and even condescended often about the flotsam he'd entertained, from local dive, to posh eatery. Hated them, loved them, laughed with them, cried for them, and, during moments of discretionary weakness, occasionally charmed selected members of the female sector into his home, and out of their clothes. Additionally, the business he was about to vacate had pulled him out of the fiscal fire more than once. The paychecks had always been bankable and, oh, but would he miss those ready-cash tips.

Jonny'd never had, much less, held an eight-to-five job. The concept, like impending marriage nuptials, was a bit unnerving. But now, after all the classroom instruction and internships, he was fully trained, or so said the certificate, to don a new hat. No full time work awaited Jonathon, as he spring-boarded himself from behind the bar, thus, he had no idea where he'd land, but resumes were well-circulated, and one surely would catch the eye of a discerning senior partner.

In his own tradition of bucking tradition, and to appease a need to align himself with an earthier, more grounded social sector, Jonny walked one of his resumes into the legal clinic for a battered women's shelter. The clinic was open to any victim of a violent household, who needed low or no cost legal assistance, and sponsored by the shelter, which also provided most of its clients.

"Do you have a car?" asked Heidi, the director of the clinic. A thirtyish woman, of slight frame, with tangled brown hair, she studied Jonathon's resume from behind a desk, pausing for the infrequent gulp from a quart bottle of water, followed by an immediate, unabashed belch. If the burps were intended to help him feel at ease, they worked.

"I do."

"Good. Maybe you can work more than one clinic. We have three a week, at different locations. You do understand this is a hundred percent pro bono, don't you?"

"I guess I do now. No matter, I'll treat it like an internship. I can always use the intake and court filing experience."

"You'll get plenty of that. I'll have to run this by the shelter's board of directors, and get back to you. We've never had a male volunteer before, but I think it's high time we did. You know, a sort of gentle reminder for shelter clients that balanced, non-violent men actually do exist. I don't think there'll be any problems. Why don't you gimme a call in a few days?"

The board approved. After only a few minutes of precise training, Jonathon worked all three clinics, at three hours per, during the week that followed.

"We're only about restraining orders. DVPA or civil harassment. Nothing else," Heidi explained, then continued, "We can do an income and expense declaration if they want support, but we're not equipped to handle divorce petitions or anything related. They have to get their own attorney for that. And they know all this, coming in. You should ask if they intend to get a divorce, though. It helps to include it in the declaration.

"You fill out the forms in longhand, based on the information they give you, then give it all to Rachel. She types it up, makes copies, and delivers it to the courthouse. Tell the clients to come back in a week, to the day, and pick up their signed paperwork."

"Signed?"

"By the judge. If he signs the application for TRO, there'll be a court date included, and that's when he makes the ruling on a more permanent order.

"A lot of the walk-in clients never come back for their paperwork. You'll just have to get used to that. There's nothing we can do about it."

Between opinions, law reporters and written motions, ad infinitum, judges necessarily do a lot of reading. Knowing that, and the fact Rachel had to type up all those declarations, Jonny thought a little economizing, amid his legal translation of various horror stories, might prove helpful toward a favorable judgment.

0-0-00: Defendant broke my nose, loosened two teeth and pushed me from a moving vehicle. ER report attached, exhibit B; police report filed.

0-0-00: Defendant, while intoxicated, threw chair through window, spraying our three year old daughter with glass chards, then knocked me to the floor and kicked me repeatedly, breaking three ribs. Police called by neighbors; arrest report on file. ER report attached, exhibit C.

0-0-00: Defendant, while intoxicated, forced me, at gun point, to have sex with two of his friends, in lieu of money he owed them for drugs. Defendant has stated on numerous occasions that he will kill both me and our daughter, should I attempt to leave him.

Jonathon's condensation of the declarations was appreciated by Rachel, whom, after about a week, thanked him for it. He noticed, during the same time frame, as he felt more comfortable in the all-female environment, that Heidi had not been present at any of the clinics. Then, on a Sunday, there was a call from Rachel.

After some small talk, she unloaded, "Heidi was in a pretty bad car accident last week."

"Oh, no."

"Yeah. She won't be back on her feet for at least six months."

"Sounds bad."

"She can't walk or feed herself. Unfortunately, there was a certain amount of brain damage. Listen, that's only half the reason I called. We're in kind of a bind now, and since you're a paralegal, and the closest thing we have to an attorney, the board says we can put you on payroll, starting tomorrow. The pay is nine dollars an hour, plus mileage and expenses."

"Okay, but I'm not sure how much help I can be."

"Oh, you'll do fine. The clients and volunteers all like you, and your forms are easy to read. Just the facts, right?"

"Right. So, what are my new duties?"

"Not that much more, really. You and I can split the typing duty. You'll have to make court filings and pick up the paperwork. Oh, and help us out on court day. That's always on Friday. It sounds like a lot, but it shouldn't add up to more than fifteen or twenty hours a week. So – interested?"

"Sure. I'm just sorry I had to get on payroll this way."

"We should have a new attorney in about a week, but you can stay on payroll if you want. The Super Bowl's coming up in a few months and we need all the help we can get."

"For the Super Bowl?"

She laughed, "No, for the week after. It's the busiest week of the year."

Once acclimated, the job became easier and the hours, as

promised, shorter. Jon's Sundays were spent at home, typing forms and declarations; Mondays, at the local copy center, where the clinic had an account; then delivering the the completed forms to two courthouses, in two counties. The twenty five cents a mile they were paying was nontaxable, and, like tips had once been, a handy little safety net. At some point, he did ask himself if he was profiting from the misfortunes of others. Since this wage could hardly be called a profit, Jonathon had to say no.

Heidi's prediction that many walk-in DVPA (Domestic Violence Prevention Act) clients would not return to pick up their paperwork, had rung quite true. So much so that it began to annoy Jonathon. Many of their declarations had read like scripts for bad horror movies, and contained 'kick-out' requests, ultimately granted by the court. In other words, their abusers could now be removed, forcibly if necessary, from the couple's home, by the Sheriff's Department. Why then would the victim not follow up? The prevalent answer was right before him, contained in declarations he'd personally typed. "He came back home and promised he'd never hit me or the kids again, and I believed him. He even brought flowers. But then, a month later, it all started again."

That passage was from the statement of a woman who *did* come back for her paperwork.

"Once burned, twice shy," she quipped during her initial intake, as Jonathon took notes. While her two children, ages three and five, played close by, she calmly, in near business fashion, laid it all out for the court to peruse. How she'd given him second chance after second chance, until it now came down to this, adding, "There's no hope for my husband, unless he gets professional help, and since he doesn't believe he has a problem, plaintiff doubts that will ever happen."

As a matter of course, Jon asked, without a thought, "You'll be filing a divorce petition, then?"

"I don't know. I can't seem to make up my mind."

"Oh? Why hesitate?"

Her face became red and contorted, as tears suddenly rolled out of her eyes and off her flushed cheeks. Now sobbing uncontrollably, the once rigid, all-business conveyor of the facts could only respond, "Because he's my honey pie."

Jon hadn't see that coming, but it was another lesson learned that should have been obvious from the start. Note to himself: all relationships are hard to end. From this point on, try a little less business and a lot more tact.

When the woman returned for her signed paperwork, the following week, she was, again, all business, but there was a hardness about her, not present before.

"You got your kick-out," Jon reported as he handed her the packet.

"Oh, fantastic, we can go home now."

"Okay, well, congratulations," he said, pointing to a flier they included with all packets, the first line of which read CONGRATULATIONS ON TAKING CONTROL OF YOUR

LIFE! Jon then instructed, "You can have him served by a process server. With the kick-out, though, you'd be better off having the Sheriff serve it. It cost twenty five dollars, but it's worth the peace of mind, and they'll make sure he's gone before you move back in."

"Yeah, I'll do that. He wouldn't dare fuck with them. He only likes to beat up girls."

With that, she stood and turned toward her babies, who'd fallen asleep on the couch, "Okay, you guys, let's go home." And then to Jon, "We got a lot of pictures to burn."

Court or 'hand-holding' days, as Rachel called them, were one part drama, two parts theater and five parts relief. Though they didn't literally hold anyone's hand, their presence was, in most cases, a matter of much needed support. There was Jonathon, Rachel, Karen, the new clinic attorney, sometimes Gail, the lead counselor from the shelter, who'd also been present at a third of the clinics, and four or five frightened clients. They were facing their batterers for the first time since they'd had them removed from their homes. It's a safe wager that neither plaintiff nor defendant had slept well the night before.

The judgments in each case seemed to have a common theme. After a few questions from the Bench, mostly for the defendant, the judge calmly directed, "I'm going to extend the order for six months and make it mutual. During that time, we'll get a recommendation from Family Court Services regarding custody and visitation. When you come back, I'll make a final ruling."

Occasionally, His Honor would include the caveat, "The Court feels both parties should also seek appropriate counseling, whether they wish to save the marriage or not."

Less frequently, counsel for the defense may make an inane request, such as, "Your Honor, the defendant fears for the safety of his pet alligator lizard, and requests that he be allowed to re-enter the premises, with civil stand-by, to retrieve and care for the alligator."

"I don't have a problem with that. Objections?"

"None, Your Honor," Karen responded, "Plaintiff defers to the alligator."

After a typical three hour clinic, while packing up the homework and engaging Gail, the middle aged, easy going counselor, in some smalltalk, Jonathon asked her what life was like, inside the shelter.

"It's like mash," she responded quickly, as though this wasn't the first time the question had been asked and answered.

"Mash?"

"Yeah, you know. The TV show."

"Oh, M*A*S*H."

"Exactly. When you deal with life threatening situations, day in and day out, a sense of humor is a must. Call it a sort of sanity maintenance tool. And it doesn't hurt for it to be occasionally off center. You should come by sometime. Meet some clients, and maybe play a little poker with the staff."

The Super Bowl came and went. Perhaps because a local team had won it, the anticipated spike in clinic clientèle never happened.

To Jonathon, Rachel was a living example that sizing up anyone, based on appearances, can be a lesson in wrong numbers. A wiry, late twenties Asian woman, with a butch type buzz cut, that was starting to grow out, and a mind for details, Rachel would have made a formidable lawyer. Not only was she a sports fan, she and her husband made a yearly pilgrimage to attend all of the Arizona spring training games of their favorite major league baseball team.

Prior to her departure for the spring training camp, Rachel asked Jon, "Any autographs I can get for you?"

"Yeah. The broadcaster," he responded, with some conviction.

"You're kidding. The announcer?"

"That's the guy. Most of the players come and go, but I grew up with 'Tell it goodbye!' And he says it now, the same way he said it thirty years ago. The guy's a home town fan, just like us."

"Okay, okay, point made, I'll see what I can do."

A month later, Rachel returned home empty handed, but not for lack of trying. "We found out what bar he drinks in, and what time he goes there, but he never showed up. We waited for three hours. We even went back the next night. Sorry."

"Not to worry, Rachel. You were sweet to do that much. Thanks for trying."

Thanks wasn't the half of it. With her dedication, humor, work ethic, mind for details, and a baseball fan, to boot, if Rachel hadn't already been married and with child, Jonathon, the lifetime sworn bachelor, would have married her himself.

Management Fabric

Pick it up here,
Put it down there.
Do your job right,
Talk back if you dare.

Don't question my reasons,
Lest I write you up.
You'll never make points
With this management pup.

Do all the grunt work,
Get dirty, get blue.
Six months down the road
You'll be up for review.

I dictate this flock,
I'm numero one.
I'm management fabric,
Experience: none.

Freedom of the Road

Outlined below are ten easy steps for the operation of a motor vehicle in the Golden State. They're from a DMV handbook I've never seen, though I'm convinced exists, as I've seen too many drivers follow these steps to believe otherwise.

1. Do not look either way, simply back out into a busy street at warp speed.

2. When using a cell or car phone, make the operation of your motor vehicle your lowest priority.

3. Do not signal when about to turn or change lanes. Your plans for the immediate future are nobody's business but your own.

4. Rear view mirrors are not intended for safety purposes. They are for you to check makeup, comb hair, or to make eye contact with the passengers in the back seat. Use them accordingly.

5. Always follow the vehicle ahead of you as closely as possible, especially at high speeds. This will be a handy maneuver in dense fog or heavy rain. Hopefully, your phone conversation

will have ended by the time the vehicle stops suddenly, and you're killed instantly.

6. Acceptable speeds are: very fast for younger drivers and very slow for older drivers. Posted speed limits are for amusement only.

7. When approaching a four way stop, while eating a hamburger, you have the right of way. Simply cruise through the intersection, without a so much as a slow-down. Other drivers will understand, as will the courts, in the event you survive.

8. Tossing items from your vehicle, such as fast food wrappers, lit cigarettes, disposable diapers, bottles, cans, etc., is recommended for the continued beautification of your vehicle's interior.

9. When pulled over by police, on suspicion of DWI, always remember the standard response, "I only had one drink."

10. When stopped for any other reason, by a Highway Patrol officer, remember to conduct yourself in a defensive, belligerent manner. S/he has only stopped you to needle you, and to generate revenue for the state, *not* because you've been operating a motor vehicle with your head placed squarely up your ass.

Empty Rooms

California's high tech boom of the late 1990s meant success for just about anyone with a computer and half a brain. If you were tech savvy, and possessed of a reasonable sphere of business acumen, a dot com had become the logical key to unlimited wealth.

Such was the case for Marla Blane, a recent business school graduate, and consistent failure at pretty much anything she endeavored, on up to graduation day. Marriage (divorced), motherhood (miscarried), real estate (no sales), even prostitution, when she envisioned herself a high priced call girl, but was stopped short by her first trick, a benevolent, older gentleman, with a badge.

Now in her early forties, Marla was armed with a diploma and a natural talent for keeping up with the evolution of desk top computers and their related software, almost daily. She had a vision, for which the bank, given her laughable credit history, was surprisingly eager to lend her money. Perhaps a bit too eager.

Way back in high school was where Marla had first befriended Susan. Inseparable gal pals that they'd become since then, it seemed only natural that Marla would approach Susan to partner with her, in her new, failure-proof business venture, "Cashlinks.com." The idea was simple. They promised instant cash, for minor emergencies -- car repair, home improvement, etc. – to be paid back at 20% interest, and all subject to a ten dollar set-up fee. The set-up fees, by themselves, when imposed on customers from New York to California, should bring hundreds of thousands of dollars, in the first month alone. To Marla, it all looked great, on paper.

Conversely, Susan was only cautiously optimistic, as evidenced during her guided tour of Marla's newly purchased condo. Purchased with moneys, as yet, wholly unrealized.

As an excited Marla showed Susan around her new, mostly empty purchase, oblivious to her distant mood, "And the love seat can go right here, and I think I'll get a few of those--"

Finally aware that Susan wasn't with her, Marla continued, "Velvet Elvis's. No, what the hell, velvet Elvis's all around. Every room in the house. Whadda ya think? Suz?

Susan snapped out of it, sort of, "Huh? Well, yeah, that might work."

Marla laughed; Suz, bewildered, responded, "What? What?"

"What planet are you on, Suzeramma? You just approved a condo full of velvet Elvis's!"

"I did? Well – look, Marla, this is all very nice, but are you sure you can afford it, in the long haul? We're doing great right now, but it's only our first month --"

"Not just great. Upwards from three thousand hits a day."

"I just don't want to see you get in over your head. I mean, what if something happens?"

"That's my Susan, ever the practical thinker. Will you stop worrying? We're set till 2006, at the earliest. You should be picking out velvet Elvis's for your own condo! Enjoy the ride! Am I right?

As Susan pondered, Marla prodded, "Work with me here, baby."

Reluctantly, Susan gave in, "Sure. Sure you're right. So, now show me where the poker playing dog pictures go."

"In the trash, next to the king. Come on, check out the master bedroom."

The master bedroom was large and as yet empty, with a panoramic view of the city. Marla had pre-set a camera on a tripod that faced the window with the best view. Susan was confused, "What's all this?"

"Gimme a dollar. You got a dollar?"

As Susan dug into the pocket of her jeans, "Sure. What for?"

With a final dial set, Marla readied the camera. Then, as she snatched the dollar bill from Susan's hand, "You'll see. Now come on, we only have ten seconds. Here, take the other end."

As they each held an end of the dollar bill and faced the camera, with the city for a backdrop, Marla commanded, "Smile and say success!"

The camera flashed as the two business partners happily declared, "Success!"

And successful they became. For about six months. Hired forty employees, with a manager for each department; leased a truckload of new, updated computers, loaded with the appropriate software; gave themselves weekly raises, and Marla, after prematurely rewarding herself with a new Mercedes, gave Susan an equally new Harley -- something Suz had fantasized over since high school -- for her birthday.

But then, as the high tech boom that had created so many overnight millionaires, crashed with a vengeance, business fell off, abruptly. The overnight millionaires throughout Northern California became overnight paupers. New, split level country homes were abandoned in mid construction, while voluntary repossession of expensive foreign cars became commonplace. Meanwhile, at cashlinks.com, the workforce had dwindled to just the two bosses and about ten employees. In her office, Marla sat quietly at her desk, her head down, rested on her folded arms, not asleep, but staring straight ahead.

After a couple taps on the door, Susan entered, with a handful of past-due invoices. Without moving, Marla defeatedly instructed her to "Just put 'em with the others," then, as she sat up, added, "I don't know why we save them. They're never gonna be paid."

"When's the last time you ate or slept?"

"Who knows? Sometime in the 90s I think.

Susan started to exit, until Marla stopped her with, "Suz? I'm gonna have to take a chapter seven. You should just, you know, get out while you can. Cut your losses. Find something else."

"You don't get rid of me that easy, honey. I stay the course, whatever happens."

"You don't understand, Suz. I'm used to failing, but not with taking people – people I care about – with me. I let 'em down, Susan. I let 'em all down. I let *you* down. Promise after promise, then it's 'sorry folks, been a change in plans. We're broke. See ya sometime.'"

"Oh, knock it off. Where'd you say you went to martyr school? Look, there's either gonna be two martyrs or no martyrs, and, frankly, the latter is juuuust a little more appealing to me."

A couple weeks later, with the condo now sold and returned to its sterile, empty state, Marla sat on the floor, in a corner of the living room, naked, with only a rainbow colored quilt around her shoulders. She stared straight ahead, as she'd done in her office, and watched the morning sun peak through drawn curtains. Behind Marla, in the dining area, was only a glass top table, atop of which were half a bottle of scotch, a glass, a snub nose .38, and one bullet.

Marla wearily brought herself to her feet, let the blanket fall, and walked to the table, where she poured herself a shot of scotch. As she brought the glass to her lips, Marla stopped in mid motion, listened to the sound of Susan's Harley, outside, amid the morning commute, as it scrambled around a corner and off into the distance. After downing the shot, she meandered into the bathroom for a shower.

In what was once the reception area of cashlinks.com, sat Susan, Bob, and a young couple, all with the hope that soon, Marla would arrive with their final paychecks. Bob, a mid twenties jet setter, was one of the many managers they'd hired, though unlike the others, was proficient at software updates and virus control. His technical talents *almost* made his obnoxious personality tolerable. Today was no exception. He slowly, annoyingly drummed his fingernails on Susan's helmet, which was on a small table beside him, until an irritated Susan picked up the helmet, with, "Do you mind?"

Unmoved, Bob responded, "Why are we doing this? I mean, come on, the horse is dead, the bitch is broke, and I got better things to do than--"

"Because we said we would," Susan interrupted, then added, "Stay or leave, Bob, but if you stay, kindly spare us your whining. She'll be here."

"If I had any money, I'd bet five she won't"

Outside, Marla parked the Mercedes and, in a business suit and overcoat, entered the building and proceeded down the long hallway, toward her now defunct small business. Old Joe, who sold sandwiches from a lunch cart, paused to say "Hi, Marla," unacknowledged. He watched, with some concern, as Marla hesitated at the Cashlinks door, composed herself, pushed the door open and entered.

In the reception area, all jumped to their feet as Marla entered, then was stopped suddenly by their stares. "I guess you'd all like to be paid, so you can get the hell out of here and find real jobs. Can't say I blame you."

As she pulled sealed envelopes from her handbag and handed them out, Marla continued, "You'll find two weeks severance pay, in addition to your regular salary."

Susan, at a loss to help her friend, took a step toward Marla, but was stopped by her cold stare, directly into Susan's eyes.

"*Nobody* – jumps my ship," commanded a stern Marla, "You're all fired. And now if you'll excuse me, I'd like to be the only one here when they come for the terminals."

A lump in her throat made it increasingly harder for Marla to speak, but she managed to squeak out, "Good luck to all of you."

Marla turned toward the door labeled 'Marla Blane, CEO.' Susan followed and stepped in her path, to face her, "Marla – hey," and forcing a smile, from a face that wanted to cry, Suz continued, "How 'bout a cup of coffee and a stinker? My treat?"

"I said excuse me, Susan."

Reluctantly, Susan stepped aside. Marla continued toward her office, but then turned to face a hurt Susan. She went to her friend, threw her arms around her. Susan was quick to return the embrace. Being about a head taller than Marla, as they hugged, Susan could see the gun in Marla's handbag, which hung from her shoulder.

Following the hug, now face to face, and both battling emotions, Susan asked, weakly, "You'll keep in touch?"

"I promise," with which Marla turned to exit into her office.

"Marla?"

Marla stopped, didn't turn. Suz continued, "It's not your fault."

Marla held up one hand to wave, and used the other to point toward the suite's exit, "Please? Just me?"

The small group began to make its way out of the suite.

Now in the privacy of her office, Marla closed the door, backed against it, her arms at her side. With eyes closed, as she took a deep breath, her right hand began to reach for and lock the doorknob. In the outer office, Susan quickly turned her attention toward the click of the lock on Marla's office door. She pondered for a second, but then became the last to exit the suite.

As the four former employees walked slowly down the hall, Bob studied his paycheck. Susan lagged a few steps behind, seriously preoccupied. Bob commented, during his perusal, "These are her personal checks. Probably aren't even any good."

"Has she ever given you a bad check, Bob?" Susan snapped.

"No, but there's always a first time."

"First time, your ass. I happen to know she took a loss on her condo, just to meet this payroll."

Susan slowed her pace to a stop, as she realized, "In fact, I think she was supposed to be out – today."

Frozen in place, Susan flashed back to the gun in Marla's handbag and the click of the door lock. She started, at a quick pace, back toward the office. Her pace became a trot, as, "Marla?"

At her desk, in the privacy of her office, Marla was hunched over, with her forehead rested squarely on the end of the gun's barrel, and her thumb on the trigger. Her chin quivered, with the final request, "Forgive me."

Out in the hallway, with the others now close behind, Susan broke into a run, "Oh, God. Marla!"

The door of the suite flew open, Susan rushed in, toward Marla's office, until she was stopped in her tracks by the sound of a single gunshot, from inside the smaller office. Hands to her mouth, Suz backed away, slowly. Bob rushed past her, tried the locked handle, then kicked the door repeatedly, until it opened. He turned quickly away, unable to deal with the sight that greeted him, from inside the CEO's office. Susan dropped to her knees. Bob knelt beside her, in an effort to comfort her, then calmly suggested to the others that they "Call nine one one."

Hours later, Susan stood alone at the threshold of Marla's office, her entry blocked by crime scene tape. She removed the tape and entered the small office, where she casually took a seat, leaned back and stared at the wall, awash with Marla's blood and brains. Softly, she whispered, "You lied to me, baby. You just fuckin' lied. Damn you."

In a hospital room, Marla could now be found, comatose, with her head wrapped in bandages. A middle aged nurse sat a few feet from the bed, and casually filed her nails. When Marla began to stir, the nurse glanced up, momentarily, from her nails.

A few groans from what could've been a bad dream, and Marla's eyes began to open. The nurse, a hardened case, again glanced at her with a dubious eye. Now fully awake, Marla felt her own face, then her head. She sat up, bewildered, "I missed?" And with her hands all over the bandages, "That's not possible. It was a --"

"Direct hit?" Nursie interrupted, continuing, "That it was, missy, that it was."

Marla plopped back down onto the pillow, "I can't do anything right."

Nursie chuckled at her patient's despair, as she stood, went to Marla's bedside, and began to adjust the head bandages. "You really wow'd 'em this time, missy. That's what you wanted, wasn't it? Go out with a bang?"

"This time? In case you haven't noticed, I'm not *out*."

"No, not entirely. I'd say you're halfway there, as per usual. But, hope springs eternal."

Nursie began to unwrap the head bandage. Marla, in a panic, "What are you – stop it!"

Marla tried desperately to stop her. Nursie slapped her hand away with, "Now, now, Nursie knows best."

With a final tug, Nursie pulled the bandage free, to reveal Marla's unscathed head. Marla, now in a full panic, grabbed her head, "My God, what have you done?" Still holding her head with both hands, as if to hold her brains in.

Nursie produced a hand-held mirror, held it directly in front of

Marla's face. Marla, in disbelief, took the mirror, held it at various angles, looking for a wound, finding none. "Damnit, I know I – wait a minute, this is no hospital."

"Nothing gets by our Marla," Nursie quipped, as she went to the window and pulled the draw string to open the curtain, which exposed the cosmos, outside. "I, uh, brought you up here so we could have some privacy. We need to talk, little girl."

Now at the window, having ignored Nursie's suggestion, Marla realized, aloud, "I finally made it. Next stop, the next dimension."

"Pay attention, hon. I said halfway there."

As she picked up a clipboard, attached at the foot of the bed and thumbed through the pages, Nursie continued, "Marla, Marla, Marla. What are we going do with you?"

"We?"

"Don't play dumb with me, missy, you know the drill by now." And as she studied the clipboard notes further, "We seem to have a pattern developing. Resourceful, but lazy little female consistently finds the easy way in *and* out of lifetimes. Never really gets it before checking out, thereby denying herself the final journey."

As Marla fell back onto the bed, "I'm so tired. What the hell's it gonna take?"

Nursie chuckled again, picked up the TV remote, "Let's review, shall we?"

She pointed the remote at the in-room TV. The screen filled with an image of, "Diana Barrymoore, 1942's most sensational new screen personality."

Marla pulled the bed covers up to just under her wide open, frightened eyes, as Nursie continued, "Wrote a book about your life of drinking and drugging. Undoubtedly helped a lot of people you never even met. Can you deny this is you, missy?"

Still wide eyed, Marla shook her head no. Nursie went on, "Pretty impressive, doll face. They even made a movie out of the book."

"Dorothy Malone played me," Marla interjected.

"You were *more* than halfway there. Then, one little setback, and you take yourself out of the game. Again."

Distraught, Marla turned on her side to face the wall. Nursie pointed and clicked the remote, at which the TV screen filled with a self portrait of Vincent van Gogh. She tapped Marla's shoulder and commanded, "Pay attention, Mr. van Gogh."

Marla peeked over her shoulder at the screen, then bolted upright, "Hey, now that's not fair! I was sick! I mean, you would've killed yourself too, if you had --"

"Nine hundred paintings and eleven hundred drawings?"

"-- and nobody gave a shit."

"Oh, they gave a shit. You were just too busy feeling sorry for yourself to notice."

With that, Nursie pointed and clicked one more time, which brought up the image of a bust of Cleopatra. "Here's an oldie, but a goodie. Cleopatra, the Seventh, Queen of Egypt. Married four times by age twenty one," she glanced, a bit puzzled, at Marla, "including two brothers?"

"I was bored, they were there, end of story."

"Produces four children. None by the brothers. And when a little thing like an attack on the homeland occurs, our diminutive darling takes the easy way out."

"Hello, we got our asses kicked."

"Is fame or good fortune so important to you that a few hard knocks along the way are just completely out of the question?"

"And I've had my hard knocks, thank you."

Nursie laughed heartily, but then got dead serious, "Have you ever been a wage slave, in a dead end job? Do you even know what the minimum wage was, last time you checked out?"

She then flipped the channel to an image of planet Earth, seen from deep space, whereupon, Nursie delivered the news Marla didn't want to hear, "You'll have to go back."

"Forget it."

"You know the alternative."

"Look I am not going through that grief again, so you can just go back and tell your superiors, or whoever perpetrates that earthbound charade, they can talk to the hand, 'cause missy ain't listening."

With that, Nursie had lost her patience. She grabbed Marla's shoulders, and, with teeth clenched, eye to eye and nose to nose, "My superiors don't like bad news, so I don't give it to them. And as for the grief, you don't experience nearly as you *cause*."

She grabbed Marla's chin and turned her head to face the TV, where Susan's image filled the screen, with the desperate request, "You'll keep in touch?"

The image of Susan on the screen now frozen, Nursie let go of Marla's chin and straightened up, as she asked, "So, what's it gonna be?" Pointing to the window, "Your own eternal playground?"

The shades dropped suddenly, as Nursie continued, "Or a graveyard in Hackensack?"

After a few moments of reflection, Marla acquiesced, "Okay, okay. One more time. But I wanna choose --"

"You're not getting this, are you, sweetheart? You've used up way too many lifetimes to have a say in anything. I had to pull some serious strings just to get you this last chance. It's my way or the highway, honey!"

"Then, on second thought, I'll take the alternative. I hear good things about fertilizer."

Nursie had opened the door to the cosmos, which floated serenely by. "Too late. Now, come on, it's all been arranged. And hey, did I mention? You'll still be a woman in charge."

She took Marla by the arm, escorted her to the opened door, with Marla offering slight resistance.

"Just hold your nose and jump," came Nursie's sound advice, while Marla struggled more aggressively against her grip, to no avail.

Now in a panic, Marla protested, "No! I won't go, and you can't make me!"

Desperate for anything to grasp, Marla clutched at Nursie's stethoscope, just before Nursie gave her a final shove out the door and into the cosmos, where she free-fell toward the Earth.

"I wouldn't bet on it, hon," was Nursie's farewell, to which she added, as she gazed out at the cosmos, from the door's threshold, "Write when you get work."

From behind a door marked 'store room,' in the Hard Knox Burger Barn and Billiard Lounge, somewhere in the Pacific Northwest, a thunderous crash was heard. The crash was followed by breaking glass and numerous large items, which avalanched onto the floor. Susan, now a food server, clad in jeans, white top, neckerchief and a name tag, approached the door, opened it, slowly, and peered in. "Marla?"

In the store room, a large, multi layer shelf rack had fallen over. Marla gingerly found her way out from under its contents of condiments, pots, pans and other culinary supplies. She wore the same food service garb, including name tag, which also stipulated, in caps, *manager.* Susan went quickly to her and began to help her up and out from under the mess, while declaring, quite matter-of-factly, "Marla, you could have been hurt!"

Marla tried to hide her shock at seeing Susan, as she responded, "Could've, hell, I think I broke my stomach."

"What are you doing with that?"

Marla looked down at the stethoscope in her hand, then, in a panic, at the name tag pinned to her blouse. She then shot a hateful look, skyward, and growled, "Nursie."

"What? Who's Nursie?"

"She's --"

In the cosmic hospital room, Nursie, with the TV remote, hurriedly scrolled through an onscreen menu display, arriving at *past life memories – on/off.* She highlighted the *off* option, then turned off the set. Back in the presumed real world, Marla then continued, "-- I don't know."

Susan attempted to take her arm and help Marla to her feet, until, "It's all right, Susan. I can manage."

"Oh. Well, okay then. The cowboys are here, and you know them, they only want their coffee from you."

As the two began their exit to the floor of the restaurant, an exasperated Marla noted, "Horny old bastards just wanna look down my top."

"What's the matter with *my* top?"

In the dining room, behind the bar, as Marla gathered cups for the cowboys, Bob, now a waiter, approached her from behind, with, "Let me help you with that, Marla."

"Thanks, Bob, I think I can handle four coffees, but if you need something to do, there's a mess in the store room. And the cowboys could probably use a boot polish."

"Sorry, just trying to help."

"Of course you are."

Hours later, her shift now complete, Marla emerged from the rear door of the rustic eatery, a small back pack slung over one shoulder. She walked by an old style girls' bicycle, with a flat tire, then into the parking lot, toward a Mercedes, identical to the one driven during the other lifetime.

Susan rushed out the same back door and ran to catch up, "Hey, Marla? Glad I caught you. Do you think me and my bike could have a ride? I mean, if it's not too much trouble? Flat tire."

Now at the Mercedes, Marla stopped, but didn't turn, annoyed at the prospect of Susan's company. In this lifetime, Marla's attitude toward Susan was one of mere tolerance. Suz was possessed of a genuine wide eyed naivete, that had endeared her to many, though up to now, had only tried the patience of Marla.

Resigned, pulling keys from the backpack, "Sure," was Marla's brief replay. She stared at the Mercedes, as did Susan, now at her side. "Nice, huh?" commented Marla.

"Yeah, I guess."

The two continued on to an older, clunker of a Toyota wagon, parked a few spaces down, where Marla unlocked the driver's side door and climbed in.

Old Joe, now a cook, dressed in kitchen whites, stood just outside the back door, where he lit a cigarette. Marla's car, on its way out, stopped in front of Joe. He obligingly opened the rear door of the car, then loaded the disabled bicycle into the back seat.

On a rural country road, Marla's car pulled into a long, straight driveway that led to an old style, run down, abandoned Spanish mansion. Off to the side of the mansion was a much smaller building, hidden by a few palm trees. Perhaps a caretaker's cottage in its day, the little house was now Susan's home. Marla's car rolled to a stop, near the front door. As the motor idled and Susan unloaded her bike, Marla, from behind the wheel, stared into the side view mirror, at the huge, silent mansion. "So, when they gonna bulldoze this place, anyway? Put up a mall or something."

"Well, Marla!" Susan pleaded, as she closed the rear door, then leaned down to address Marla, eye to eye, "Did you hit your head or something, when you fell in the store room? You know this is my home."

"Oh, yeah. Sorry."

"But since you brought it up, maybe you noticed, they're trying to sell it. And I know whoever buys it ain't gonna need a caretaker. Heck, they'll probably do just what you said," and as she glanced over at the run down building, "bulldoze it. Hey, you wanna come in and have ice cream? I got some rocky road."

"Oh, no thanks, I've got a – ya know, hold me back."

Inside Susan's unpretentious studio cottage was a couch, coffee table, rocking chair and wood stove. Curiously, empty picture frames decorated the wall, opposite the couch where Marla sat. As Susan entered from the kitchen, two heaping bowls of ice cream in hand, "I had big plans for this place when I moved in. Maybe it's better this way."

"Plans? For this?"

"Well, sure, I mean I was gonna put another window there, and a few of my pictures there --"

"Wait. Pictures? What kind of pictures?"

Susan glanced sheepishly over at something on the floor, covered by a blanket, near a wall. Marla set the bowl down on the coffee table, went to the mystery blanket, cautiously lifted it to reveal five or six unframed paintings, in a row that leaned against the wall. Amazed at the find, she knelt beside it and slowly thumbed through the paintings, her perusal punctuated by the occasional awe struck glance at Susan. "You did these?" Susan nodded, in wary anticipation, as Marla continued, "They're beautiful. All these years, I had no idea."

"Well, silly, you shoulda come in for ice cream sooner. Doncha know? So – you like 'em, then?"

"Like's not the word for it," as she held a painting at arm's length, "Where?"

"Huh? Oh, you mean where do I paint? Over in the big house. I got sort of a little studio set up. It gets real good light through those big windows." Now much more relaxed and relieved at Marla's adoration of her work, Susan added, "Daddy says it's an outlet for me."

"Like a sexual outlet?"

"I guess. He might be right. I do get a little tingly under my pants when I'm in an art supply store. But you know, he also says I shouldn't try to be a show off, so I figure, heck, just paint these old things and, you know, be happy with what I did."

Still intrigued by the paintings, Marla countered, "Yeah, well, I'm no art critic, but I think dear old daddy missed the call this time."

"Hey, ya know, I had this idea."

As Marla got comfortable on the floor and resumed eating the ice cream, "Do tell."

"Promise not to laugh? I never told anyone about this because it might be dumb or something."

"Scout's honor, no laughing."

"Well," Excitedly, Susan quickly sat on the floor, next to Marla, and continued, "you know those bed and breakfast things, where people just come and sleep over, then you feed 'em in the morning and get 'em out, and start on a new batch?"

Marla nodded, mildly interested, as Suz continued, "Maybe I could be the one who buys this property, and then I could fix up the old mansion and make a bed and breakfast thing, and if people liked my pictures --"

"Paintings."

"-- paintings, they'd wanna buy one while they were here. Oh, I couldn't get rich or anything, but gee wiz, wouldn't that be fun?"

"Might. Just might. However, there is the little matter of money."

"Yeah, that's sorta where the fantasy ends. But I got some saved up, and maybe if I asked daddy, he'd wanna help."

"Daddy again."

"Or maybe – you?"

Outside, about an hour later, as Marla got into, and started the clunker, declaring, "I'll think about it," Susan waved from her porch.

Marla turned the car around, began to drive out, but then slowed to a stop and backed up, toward the mansion. After getting out of the car, she walked, slowly, hands on hips, toward the front porch. She tried the locked door, then went to a nearby window where, with hands shielding the daylight, Marla peered in to have a look around.

The empty living room she saw was spacious, with a giant fireplace and chimney, surrounded by endless hardwood floors. Marla's fertile imagination placed Susan's paintings on the walls, one by one, in their frames. Her reality was then sharply distorted by intermittent flashbacks of the empty cashlinks.com office. Marla, in somewhat of a trance, turned to face Susan, now at her side.

"Are you all right?" Susan inquired.

"I'm fine. Thanks. I had sort of a – dream, I think."

"But your eyes were open, so you weren't sleeping. Daydreams, maybe, huh? Daddy says too many of those, and you've probably got something. You know, like ringworm."

A spirited laugh snapped Marla out of the trance, "Yeah, that's it, I got worms! I have got to meet your daddy."

Bewildered, Susan forced a chuckle, "Was that funny?"

"In its own little way."

Back in her car, Marla started the engine, which sputtered. "Thanks for the ice cream, kiddo. You are a sweet one."

Marla revved the engine, loudly, to keep it started, during which time Susan saw the opportunity to impart, "You're sweet too, Marla. And I love you. I love you so much, it hurts."

With the engine back down to an idle, "What?"

"Nothin'. Bye, Marla," was all Susan could muster up, at which Marla waved and drove off.

That evening, as Marla sat alone at the kitchen table, in her apartment, she tapped the keys of a pocket calculator. After perusing a small bank book, she tapped out a few more numbers on the calculator, then stared at the total, leaned her head back and stared at the ceiling. "I could do this."

A few days later, at the Hard Knox, with the lunch rush mostly over, the cowboys shot a game of pool, while Bob and Susan cleaned the dining tables. Lester, the mid sixties, alcoholic owner of the establishment, slept peacefully, passed out at one of the tables. As Marla, ledger in hand, breezed by Joe's cooking corner, "Blues night tonight, Joe. We ready for it?"

"I got twenty dead chickens at the ready, doll face."

A hopeful Susan approached Marla to inquire, "Did you wanna talk or something?"

"As a matter of fact, I do," but then, after a glance over at Lester, "I need to put Sleeping Beauty to bed first. See you outside?"

"Okay, see ya then."

"Uh, hey, Marla," Bob chimed in, "Why don't you go ahead? I'll take care of Lester."

At first, possessed of the knowledge that Bob's sites were set firmly on her job, Marla was ready to snarl at the suggestion. But then, an *idea*. She gave him a friendly, albeit, phony pat on the back, which preceded an even phonier, "Sure, Bob, that's really sweet of you. Thanks ever so much."

"Think nothing of it, always glad to help."

Outside, Marla caught Susan, as the latter was about to mount her bicycle.

"So Suz, tell me, think you might like having me for a landlord?"

Susan's big eyes got bigger, "Would I! Really, Marla, really?"

"Talked to the agent this morning. Let's hold off on any celebrating till we see if I can qualify."

"You'll qualify, I know you will. Whatever that is. Oh, Marla, it'll be so fantastic! Hey, and I'm real good at picking things out, so I could pick out some curtains for you."

"For us. I can't do this alone."

Marla shot an anxious glance toward the rear exit of the restaurant, as she continued, "Look -- you go ahead home, I'll catch up later. And save me some ice cream. Sound like a plan?"

"Yeah, that's a really good plan. See you later."

As Susan peddled off, Marla refocused her attention on the rear exit of the building. Inside, Bob propped up a near-comatose Lester, as he struggled to walk the inebriate toward the exit. Lester's drunken ramblings were barely audible, until he raised his voice to inquire, "Where's that bitch, Marla? This is her job!"

"I dunno, boss," Bob responded, "I turned around and she was gone. No worries, though. I'll get you home, safe and sound."

"I oughta fire that bitch, too. Hell, you're all fired. I'll run the whole goddamn show, all by my goddamn self."

Under the watchful eye of Joe, from his corner, Bob chuckled, as he pushed the back door open for Lester.

Since Lester's lair was only out the back door and up a flight and a half of outdoor stairs, Bob, or whomever's job it was, on any given day, didn't have far to go, after which, the deed would be swiftly in the past. Bob stood at Lester's doorway, where he bade the soon to be unconscious business owner farewell, and pulled the door shut. Then, feeling accomplished and in all the right graces, he bounced happily back down the stairs. At the foot of the stairs, Bob turned toward the parking lot, but was frozen by the sound of Marla's voice, "A little guy talk, there, Bob?"

Marla strolled casually from under the stairwell. Bob, feigning virtue, looked right, then left, "Me?"

"Not your twin sister."

He walked slowly toward Marla, "So, Marla! How's it going?"

As she grabbed the front of his shirt and threw him against the nearest wall, "Swimmingly, Bob."

Withe her left hand, Marla kept hold of Bob's shirt, while she slammed her right palm into his crotch, grabbed hold of his goods and squeezed, for all she was worth, "I thought you and I might have a little chat, too."

Bob's mouth was wide open, but between the fear in his head and the pain in his groin, that radiated throughout his body, his voice was gone.

Marla calmly continued, "Don't think I don't know what you're up to, ya old smoothie. Better men – *much* better men than you have tried and failed. Now, you can kiss Lester's ass till his hat flies off, but, see, I've got pocket aces, and if you're as smart as that drunken slob thinks you are, you won't ask me to show those aces, 'cause baby, they never lose, not even to a Royal."

As she tightened her grip on his groin, Marla had to inquire, "Are we understood?" Bob's voice had returned, but only managed a groan, at which Marla inquired, "Is that a yes?"

He nodded. Marla then let go of him and backed off a few steps to chirp, "Good. See you for blues night?"

Bob, bent over, his face contorted in pain, looked up, helplessly, at Marla, who innocently cocked her head, with a somewhat exaggerated, toothy grin.

A few hours later, Marla's car pulled to a stop near the front porch of the broken down mansion. As she got out of the car, she noticed Susan's bicycle on the porch, and the huge front door, ajar. From inside, piccolo music could be heard. Marla followed its audio path.

Dwarfed by the immenseness of the empty living room, Susan sat in the middle of the floor, on the rainbow colored quilt, where she played the piccolo, without interruption. Her big eyes followed Marla, who entered the room and crossed to the oversized, floor level fireplace hearth, where she quietly took a seat and listened. Suz finished the solo, after which she smiled up at her heroine.

"All this time I know you," Marla mused, "and all I thought you could do was sling hash."

"I felt some not-so-great leftover karma, so I thought I better try and, you know, cleanse it a little."

"I'm for that. With a piccolo?"

"Well, it's all I had handy. Are you sure you wanna do this, Marla? Buy this old place, I mean? It'll be an awful big --"

"Responsibility? Yeah, I know. But I'm forty five years old, and that clunker in the driveway is the only thing I've ever owned. Even if this pipe dream tanks, at least I can say I gave it my – *our* best shot. Apologies in advance, if I take you down with me."

"Oh, I don't think that'll happen. You're so smart and everything."

"Please don't say 'what could possibly happen.'"

"No, I was just gonna say how come a smart, pretty girl like you ain't married, or at least got some guy?"

"Hey, what is this, twenty questions for Marla day?"

"Come on, tell me. How come?"

"I could ask you the same thing."

"Daddy says it ain't polite to answer a question with a question."

"Score one for daddy." As she got comfortable on the hearth, Marla continued, "Marriage is an iron clad contract between two people. It requires the only license that never expires. No one's ever meant that much to me.

"Better clean up the rest of that karma, don't you think?"

Susan resumed the piccolo solo, which became second nature, as her concerned eyes watched Marla, who stretched out on her back and stared up at the ceiling. The breezy woodwind solo gently lulled Marla back into one of her trances. After a few minutes, Susan ended the tune and lowered the piccolo. She watched Marla, who, almost now in a death stare, didn't move.

"Earth to Marla."

Marla stirred, sat up, slowly, "Huh?"

"Dreams again?"

She nodded, rubbed her eyes, before Susan asked, hedgingly, "You wouldn't wanna tell me about one of them, would you?"

"No. Not yet. It's like a story someone's telling me. But it has no ending. When it does, you'll be the first to know, I promise. So, I believe you were going to tell me about Susan's love life."

"I was? Ain't much to tell, really. I only been kissed once, and I don't even think I did that right. But, you know, he tricked me."

Marla looked at her watch, began to stand, "Into kissing him?"

"Worse than that."

Marla strolled toward the door. Susan followed, and proceeded, "After he kissed me, he unzipped his jeans and showed me his thing. It was awful big and hard and, you know, kinda purple."

Now outside, while they strolled along the porch, toward Marla's car, Suz went on, "He told me it was a sickness, and that I caused it, and if I didn't put it in my mouth, and let nature take its course, he'd have to walk around like that for the rest of his life. Well, heck, I didn't wanna be the blame for that, so I did what he told me."

"And then?"

"It wasn't so bad, I guess. The gooey stuff was a little saltier than I like, but he said it was good for me, so I just drank it down."

"Oh, gawd."

"But then, he started bringing his friends over. That sickness must've been real contagious, 'cause they *all* had it. One, after another, after another. They were coming around at all hours! Even started calling me the healer. But they were getting healed, and all I was getting was a belly ache. And no kisses."

Now at the car, Marla opened the door to get in, while she inquired, "So, what then? They stopped coming around? Forgive the pun."

"Oh, yeah, daddy set me straight. Them too."

"Daddy knows about this?"

In the car, Marla began to pull the door shut, but hesitated at Susan's stone faced, dead serious response, "Daddy knows everything."

A bit preoccupied, Marla pulled the door shut, as Susan, back to her wide eyed, inquisitive self, pitched, "Marla, you must've been kissed by a lot of guys. Did you always do it right? Is it real complicated? Looks complicated in the movies."

As Marla started the car, "No, not complicated at all. First you close your eyes, then just let nature take its course."

The car began to move, Marla reassured Susan, "Trust me, Suz, in the right time and right place, with the right person, you'll magically know all you need to know."

Susan waved as Marla began to drive out. But then, the car stopped suddenly, and Marla leaned her head out the window, "I almost forgot, can you help out, tonight? I don't think Bob's gonna make it."

"Sure. What's the matter with him?"

"I dunno, he was walking kinda funny, last time I saw him. Probably ringworm or something. See ya there?"

"Okay, Marla. Bye."

At about 2:30am, after having worked the entirety of 'blues night' and dropped off Susan and her bicycle at home, Marla, exhausted, entered her apartment. After she hit the lights on and tossed the backpack on the couch, Marla noticed a light that blinked on the answering machine. She pushed the 'play' button, on her way into another room. The robotic voice then announced to an empty room, "One message. Sent: yesterday, seven fifty five PM," after which came the voice of – "Hi, Marla, Gary Connors at Linbrook Realty, sorry I missed you. Great news, we got you qualified for the loan. Looks like your co-signer's bar'll work fine for collateral."

As Marla re-entered from the other room, and now payed close attention, the recording continued, "All you have to do is come up with the ten thousand, and we'll finance the down. The seller's agreed to carry a second. Gimme a call when you get in and --"

Marla grabbed the phone, began to dial, but then, after a glance at the clock, and the lateness of the hour, hung it up. She pondered for a few seconds, then picked up the receiver again and began to dial. And again after the first few numbers, she paused and replaced the receiver. "No, that's not the way." She grabbed her keys and quickly exited the apartment.

A few minutes later, Marla's clunker skidded to a stop at the front door of Susan's cottage. She got out of the car and walked a quick few steps toward the cottage, as a light was on inside. About to knock on the door, Marla paused at the sound of distant piccolo music. She looked over at the mansion. A small attic window was dimly lit. Guardedly, she walked toward the old building and entered a side room, where a light also burned.

While the piccolo music continued from upstairs, Marla took a slow, awestruck tour of what turned out to be Susan's art studio. Lit by a bare light bulb that hung from the middle of the ceiling, the room proudly displayed dozens more of Susan's paintings. She found her way to a single chair that faced an easel, where Marla gazed at a nearly finished portrait of herself.

In the attic, lit only by a candle on a chair, Susan was seated on the floor, on the same rainbow colored quilt. Garbed in a flannel nightgown, she played the last ten or twelve notes of her solo, lowered the piccolo and, once again, smiled up at her heroine. "Did you forget something?"

Marla sauntered closer and took a seat on the floor, facing Susan, "You might say that. I brought you some news. Sorry, no ice cream, but the news is a lot less messy."

With wide eyed schoolgirl excitement, Susan commanded, "Tell me, tell me!"

"Let's put it this way, I thought maybe tomorrow, you and I could drive into the city, and maybe, oh, pick out some curtains? You did say you're a pretty good picker-outer--"

"Oh my gosh! Really, Marla, really?"

"Got the call tonight. We're in, kiddo."

The two born-again teenyboppers shrieked, as Susan threw her arms around Marla. Following the embrace, as her hands remained on Marla's shoulders, "Marla, that's so fantastic! And you drove all the way over here just to tell me?"

Marla shrugged, "What are friends for?"

"This friend can't thank you enough. I mean, how do you say thank you enough, so that --"

"Shhhhh."

As Marla cleared a lock of hair from Susan's face, "First, you close your eyes."

Suz's eyes slowly closed. Marla kissed her cheek, then her parted lips. She pulled back to watch Susan, who didn't move or open her eyes. Marla kissed her again, this time, passionately. Susan slid her arms the rest of the way around Marla's shoulders, and pulled her down, as the long, passionate kiss continued.

The morning sun that streamed through the small window of the attic found our naked lovers, entwined in one another's arms, asleep on the rainbow quilt, after a full night of corporeal bliss. Marla was the first to open her sleepy eyes. She sat up and leaned back on a wall, pulling Susan up with her. As Susan awakened and snuggled closer to the warmth of Marla's flesh, came the question, "Is it too soon to say I love you?"

"I already knew. You only reaffirmed it when with that first kiss."

"How did you know?"

"I saw the painting. You don't make a perfect portrait like that of someone, without loving them."

"But it's not even finished. I was gonna give it to you for your birthday, after we opened the B&B."

"Sorry if I ruined your surprise," then, after a brief kiss, "but it was worth it. I love you back, little one. And I want to love you more. And care for you. And protect you. For the rest of our lives."

"Did we just get married?"

"If that's what you want."

"I do if you do."

"I do."

A few hours later, on a southbound freeway, Marla's clunker held its own in the lane designated for San Francisco. Inside the car, Susan, oblivious to their location, did her best to make one of her many points, "You see, when hearts connect, it's forever, no matter what kinda meat they're wearing, at any given time. It's like, ya know that river that runs behind my house? Well, the banks of the river are – well, they're *time*. And the river, it runs *through* time."

"And the river is, what? Oh, wait, I remember, the river is love."

"Exactly! And it runs through all time."

"Well, that's all hip and cool, but what happens when someone dies? Does the love just keep going?"

"Listen, in a good wrestling match, love beats death, every time. It's nature's way. Doncha know?"

"Are we talking about reincarnation?"

Susan had to think about that one, and finally, "We might be."

About an hour later, exiting the freeway in Oakland, Marla's car coasted to a stoplight at the end of a two lane offramp. Marla saw not the Mercedes, with Nursie at the wheel, that pulled to a stop beside her at the light. Staying focused on the issue at hand, Marla concluded to Susan, "I suppose anything's possible, but as for what happens after we die, sorry, sweet cake, my money's on fertilizer."

Now with a green light, an exasperated Nursie rolled here eyes, floored it, and screeched off. Marla, her attention grabbed, mused, "Wonder what his problem was."

"Her," corrected Susan.

In a garment shop, Susan and Marla, like kids in a toy shop, moved quickly from display racks to tables to hanging materials, with analytical input from each of the two 'experts' at every stop; in Jack London Village, the arm in arm lovers strolled past shops, boutiques and the scenic waterfront, en route to a patio restaurant, where they settled in for lunch.

Amid their up-tempo table chatter, after a particularly droll 'Susanism,' Marla giggled, as she picked up her wine glass and offered a toast. When she tilted her head back to drink from the glass, Marla froze at the site of herself, in the other lifetime, who stood on the third floor balcony of her posh condo, wrapped in the rainbow quilt. The doppelganger turned to look directly at Marla, who'd since lowered the wine glass, but continued her stricken gaze.

Marla shook her head violently, to which a concerned Susan inquired, "Marla? You okay?"

After refocusing on the balcony, where her double was no longer, Marla replied, "Yeah. Yeah, I'm fine. We should probably get going if we wanna beat the traffic."

On a city sidewalk, as they walked, side by side, Marla and her lover chatted about who will do what, and when. The conversation eventually led to Susan's request, "Marla, do you have any aspirin? I sorta got this headache starting."

"Too much excitement? Or was it that overpriced house wine? Sorry, babe, no aspirin, but we'll be on our way soon and you can take a nap. Where'd we park, anyway? I know it's around here, somewhere."

Susan pointed across the street, "Over there, I think."

After having crossed the street, and continuing her chatter, now at a more brisk pace, Susan discovered, upon a brief glance to her right, that she'd been talking to herself. "Marla?"

Bewildered, she looked around, then behind her, to discover Marla, who'd stopped, about thirty feet back, where she stood and stared at an office building, across the street. Susan backtracked to her side. The building that so entranced Marla was the building that had housed her business in another lifetime, Cashlinks.com.

"What are you doing?" inquired a flustered Susan.

"This place. This building. I've been here before."

"Okay, what's that they call it? Deja vu or something? Everybody has 'em. Doncha know?" As she took Marla's arm, to try and guide her, "Can we go now, Marla? This headache's getting worse."

Marla pulled away from her, with a stern assertion, "No, wait."

Now fully engrossed, Marla stepped off the sidewalk and into the street, to cross toward the building, off of which she could not take her eyes, "This can't be."

As Susan tagged along, "Are you daydreaming again? Gee wiz, Marla, this is really getting to be a problem with you."

Marla continued slowly, in her trance-like state, toward the building's entrance, while Susan reasoned, "Marla, we passed this building before. Remember? Now, come on. Please?"

At the building's entrance, Marla slowly extended her hand toward the door handle, while Susan made a final appeal, "Marla --"

Inside the area we once knew as the Cashlinks reception area, Marla looked slowly around the room, as she experienced inexplicable, momentary flashbacks of the room, when it was her flourishing business. A female receptionist looked up from her work, with a smile, which abruptly disappeared upon seeing Marla's state. "Can I – help you?"

Marla continued her visual tour of the room, to which the receptionist insisted, "Hel-lo?"

That got Marla's attention. As she shifted her stare down to the receptionist, "I don't know you," after which she resumed her pan of the room, "but I know this place."

"Come on, Marla, please!" Susan interjected.

Marla stared at a smaller office's door, which, before her eyes, became labeled, Marla Blane, CEO, a sight that thoroughly mystified her.

Suz attempted to divert the concerned receptionist, "She's harmless, I assure you. We're from out of town. Maybe you noticed that. We're not lost or anything, but we were on the road all morning, and she's just really tired and --" she looked toward Marla and raised her voice, "--we'll be leaving soon."

The diversion had worked long enough for the receptionist not to have noticed Marla, who'd inched her way toward the smaller office. As she reached for the doorknob, the receptionist intervened, "Excuse me, you can't – *excuse me!* That's a private office. Miss?"

As Marla opened the office door, the receptionist hurriedly snatched up the phone receiver, and Susan attempted a verbal restraint, "Oh, don't do that. Please. I'll get her out of here, I promise."

Susan, now in the grip of some obvious pain, massaged her temples, as she continued,"We know each other five years now, and she's never done anything like this before--"

In the smaller office, Marla stood just inside the doorway. She slowly perused the full shelves, yuppie wallhangings and unoccupied desk, which was obviously someone's workplace. Then came the sudden, inexplicable vision of the office on Cashlinks' final day. Empty shelves, packed boxes, and at the desk, her doppelganger. Terrified, Marla watched, intently, as the Marla at the desk, her head rested against the end of the gun barrel, once again made her final appeal, "Forgive me," soon after which she pulled the trigger and blew her brains onto the wall behind her.

The sound of the gunshot jarred Marla, still at the door. Her head snapped back, her eyes wide, at the shock of having just witnessed her own suicide.

Meanwhile, Susan, still busy with the diversion of the receptionist, continued to occasionally massage her own temples until, "I've even got some pictures of us at--"

She looked down, then back at the woman behind the desk. A slow stream of blood had trickled from Susan's right nostril. She rubbed her nose, looked at the blood on her fingers, which was substantial, then back at the receptionist, "Would you happen to have – a tissue?"

Susan's eyes rolled back; she then collapsed in a heap. "My God," proclaimed the receptionist, as she bolted from behind her desk.

Marla was brought back to reality by the receptionist's plea, from the other room, "Somebody help!"

As she looked toward the reception area, "Susan."

Marla rushed to, and knelt beside her comatose lover, on the floor, who now bled from her right ear and nostril. As she held Susan's hand, she attempted to soothe her, "Suz? Baby? Can you hear me? It's okay, sweetheart, you're gonna be fine. Minor setback."

The flustered receptionist interrupted, "She was talking, and started bleeding, and passed out. I didn't know what--"

Marla calmly cut in, "Could you please just get us some help?"

Minutes later, Nursie, behind the wheel of the parked Mercedes, watched, from across the street, as paramedics loaded Susan, on a gurney, into the back of an ambulance. Marla jumped in just before a paramedic slammed the door shut. With lights and siren, the ambulance cruised off. Nursie, after finishing the last of some fast food French fries, started the luxury car and drove off, in the opposite direction.

The clock in the ER waiting room read just minutes before midnight, as Marla, one of only three disparate vigil keepers present, sat and stared down at the floor, her hands clasped behind her head. When the automated 'No Admittance' door opened, and a man in a doctor's smock walked through, file folder in hand, Marla knew he was there for her, and anxiously stood to greet him.

"Marla Blane?"

"Yes."

He offered his hand, "I'm Dr. Nelson. Let's sit."

As they sat, and he thumbed through the file folder, "You're listed here as – spouse?"

"She's my wife."

"Fair enough. Your wife has had a cerebral vascular accident." With Marla at an obvious loss, he simplified, "A stroke."

Taken aback, Marla brought her hands to her face, stared straight ahead, "But she's so young."

"It can happen to anyone, for any number of reasons. You okay?"

Marla nodded slightly, "So, how bad is it? Is she paralyzed?"

"Only on her right side."

"Only?"

"Fortunately, we got to her in time with blood thinners, or she might've had total paralysis. Her speech and motor centers have extensive damage, but in time, and with proper physical therapy, she can learn to walk and talk again, almost normally. You can get together with your insurance carrier and they'll let you know what they will or won't cover --"

"Uh, we have 'you-pay'"

"I see. Well, that's not really my department, but I know the county facilities are just as thorough as any other. I can recommend a few if you like."

"No, that's okay. We're not from around here. When can she come home?"

"Couple weeks, maybe."

"Can I see her?"

"Of course," after which the two stood, and he led Marla out of the room.

In the Intensive Care Unit, Susan, on her back, with half opened eyes, was connected to I.V. Drips, oxygen mask and a heart monitor. Her head was turned left as, even in her mostly paralyzed state, she'd keep a hopeful gaze on the door. Her eyes widened and she whined softly, her tenacity having been rewarded with the sight of Marla, gowned and masked, who approached her bedside. Marla leaned in for a careful hug. With her good arm, Susan held her tight. After the embrace, Marla pulled a chair close to the bedside. After sitting, she held Susan's hand and spoke in a soft, maternal tone, "Can't take you anywhere."

Suz turned Marla's palm up, and, with her finger, printed out s-o-r-r-y in the middle of her beloved's hand.

"Hey, listen to me, kiddo, it's not your fault. Minor setback. Remember?"

Susan then printed h-o-m-e on Marla's palm, at which Marla responded, "Yeah, sweetheart, we're going home. Maybe not for a few days, till you can travel and I can make a few arrangements."

Suz became a bit agitated, Marla continued, "No county hospitals for my baby. Nothin' but the best for the best. Sound like a plan?"

Susan's big eyes and half-smile, from under the oxygen mask, agreed. Marla's reassurance went on, "Rest now. Dream sweet dreams of rocky road ice cream and dancing nymphs. It'll all look better in the morning. I promise."

S-t-a-y was the next word printed on Marla's hand. "Yeah," Marla responded. She pulled the chair closer, laid her head down on the bed, at Susan's side, "I'll stay with you."

Susan placed her hand on Marla's shoulder, while her eyes grew tired and slowly closed.

Over the next three months, Marla was able to get Susan home and situated with wheel chair and hospital bed, in her little apartment. She also hired an attendant, or 'care giver,' named Cindy, to help with Susan's daily hygiene, feeding and general companionship, when Marla couldn't be there, which, due to split shifts at the Hard Knox, was often.

One such afternoon found Marla, with the lunch rush subsided, using her backpack for a pillow, asleep at the end of the bar. The cowboys mumbled amongst themselves as they shot a serene game of pool, while Bob cleaned tables, in his usual speedy manner. A sober Lester was behind the bar. As Bob delivered a tray of dirty glasses to Lester's service bar, he thought he'd also deliver the suggestion, "Don't you think we should wake her up?"

"Nah, let her sleep," replied Lester, "Between Susan and this place, she's been running herself ragged."

About six stools down from where Marla snoozed, with her head turned in the opposite direction, three clean cut, early 30s men amiably approached the bar. "Three Buds," one of the men ordered.

"You got it," Lester responded, then turned to the beer box.

As Lester gathered the beers, with his back to them, the man continued, "You worked here a while, partner?"

"Long enough."

"We're looking for a girl they used to call the healer."

The allegedly slumbering Marla's eyes snapped open. The man added, "Kinda pretty, kinda dumb. Liked to put things in her mouth."

"Nope," Lester replied, as he set down the beers and plucked a fiver from the man's hand, "Don't know anyone like that."

As Marla rolled slowly off the barstool, and onto her feet, "There's a new healer in town."

She strolled seductively toward the men, unbuttoning her top, "Somebody here got the sickness?"

"Uh, yeah, I think we all do," replied one of the men.

"Well, we sure wouldn't want you to walk around like that for the rest of your life, now, would we?"

As she held the blouse open, exposing her bare bosoms to the men, Lester intervened, "Yeah, Marla, I really don't think --"

"Relax, Lester. Every good story has a happy ending. Isn't that right, fellas?"

"Got me happy already," one of the men sarcastically interjected, to the amusement of the others.

"Well then, waddaya say, Mr. happy man?" Marla countered, seductively. As she pointed over her shoulder, in the direction of the men's room, "Step into my office?"

With a hand on the man's back, Marla guided him toward the men's room and continued, "Let's get you all healed up, shall we?"

As the man obediently entered the bathroom, "Works for me, honey."

The door closed behind the make-believe healer and her unsuspecting charge. Dead silence prevailed, as all eyes remained on the men's room door. After about ten seconds, an agonized, male scream echoed from the other side of the door. Bob, now behind the bar, cringed.

"Damn! What the hell'd she do, bite it off?" Inquired one of the men.

"No," declared Bob, "but you're on the right track."

Marla emerged from the men's room, buttoned up and tucked in, went to the bar and snatched up her backpack. "See you for band night, Bob?" She winked at him, as she turned to leave the building.

One of the remaining men asked, "Is she the owner or something?"

"Yeah," Lester answered, "she's -- something. Another beer for ya?"

At home, Marla entered to a cluttered apartment. Susan, in her wheelchair, was being spoon-fed ice cream by Cindy. With a momentary glance at Marla, Cindy greeted, "Well, hi! We're having ice cream. Care to join us?"

"Hi, Cindy. No, thanks, maybe later," after which she went to Susan's side and knelt to make eye contact. "And how was your day?"

As Marla held her hand, Susan attempted to say something that sounded like a question.

Having perfectly understood the question, Marla answered, "No, babe, I'm just home for a few hours. Band night, tonight, remember?"

While Marla attempted to wipe drool from the corner of Susan's mouth with a bib that hung under her chin, Susan offered a low key whine of discontent. Cindy raised another spoonful of ice cream, which was promptly waved away by Susan. "Okee doke," responded Cindy, as she stood up, "we'll just save the rest for later."

After Cindy's exit to the kitchen, Marla looked again into Susan's eyes, "Be right back, okay? I need to talk to Cindy for a minute."

Suz responded with the only two words she could now say, unimpeded, "Uh huh," after which Marla kissed her cheek and left the room.

In the kitchen, as Cindy washed a few dishes, "There's a letter for you on the table, from the rehab facility. Maybe it's the one you were waiting for."

Marla opened and studied the letter, then commented, "Now, how'd they know that's all the money I have in the world?"

"Bitter sweet?"

"They can send a van to pick her up this afternoon. Start the rehab tomorrow morning. That's the good news."

"And the bad?"

"Looks like I can't afford you anymore."

"Oh, you won't need me, anyway. That place has a great staff. She'll be in good hands."

Marla picked up the phone and began to punch numbers.

A little later, with Cindy gone, Susan slept in the wheelchair, covered by the rainbow quilt, while Marla, using the top of the TV for a hard surface, hurriedly wrote out a check. A small, packed suitcase was on the floor, nearby. She tore the check from the book, set it aside, then went to Susan's side, where she once again knelt, and began to wipe Susan's face with the bib.

Susan's eyes blinked open, greeted by, "Hey, girl, that ice cream sure has a sleepy effect. You were out cold. Get it? Ice cream? Cold? Never mind."

Suz smiled her half-smile as Marla continued to clean her up and adjust her clothing. "Today's the big day, Suzeramma. Uptown rehab, here we come."

Susan protested, and tried to say *no!* Then scrawled something on a tablet in her lap. Marla watched, as she wrote *Help me die – make me die.*

"Suicide? Come on now, you know that's not an option. We still got a B&B to build. With all your paintings on the walls. And you *will* paint again." She got closer to whisper in Susan's ear, "I promise."

As Marla stood and began to commandeer the wheelchair,

"Besides, you're gonna have the best physical therapist *and* the best food."

Marla snatched up the check, stuffed it in her pocket, then picked up the suitcase and placed it in Susan's lap, as she continued, "And I'll be there every night to steal your dessert."

She opened the front door and, as they went out, "Let's wait out here, okay? Your ride'll be here any minute."

As promised, the disabled transport van arrived shortly thereafter. With Marla close by, Susan was placed on the power lift, and her chair secured. Just as the driver was about to engage the lift, Susan flew into a tantrum. She screamed, flailed her arm and kicked with her useable leg.

Marla managed to get her arms around Susan and hold her tight. She softly reassured, "We'll go together. We'll go together," while her lover now cried like a baby.

En route to the inpatient rehab facility, Susan, her wheelchair secured to the floor of the van, appeared glum, like a prisoner, en route to the big house. Marla sat close to her, on a makeshift stool, and held her hand.

That night, 'band night,' as a Chicago blues group played a strangely appropriate ballad, the mostly subdued audience seemed to reflect Marla's mood. Lester and Bob worked the bar. While Bob dried glasses, he watched Marla, from the corner of his eye. She sat alone, at a small cocktail table, near the stage, and watched the crowd. Her mind, however, was, understandably, somewhere else. Unknown to her, one of the many patrons who occupied the barstools, with their backs to the room, was Nursie.

After closing, Marla gathered empty glasses from around the room. Bob, at the bar, unloaded more empties from a tray, as Marla approached and set some glasses on it. "Thanks for helping out tonight, Bob. You're a life saver, I really mean that."

She offered her hand for a handshake. As Bob quickly covered his groin area with the tray, Marla continued, "Peace. How 'bout it?"

They shook hands and she took the tray from him, as she suggested, "Now, go on home, I'll finish up here."

"I got a better idea," said Bob, after which he set two shot glasses on the bar, filled them with whiskey, and picked one up to offer a toast.

Marla was a bit perplexed at the offer, as she eyed the lone shot on the bar, but then surrendered to the spirit of the offer, "What the hell."

They toasted and drank the shots in one gulp. Marla set her glass down and began to go back toward the tables, when Bob stopped her with, "She'll be okay, Marla."

She turned and slowly climbed a barstool, as, "No. No, I don't think so. She talked about suicide today."

"Hmm. Long term solution to a short term problem."

Marla, a bit struck by Bob's astuteness, responded, "That's right.

Did I miss something here? Last time I checked, the only thing you were sensitive about was getting my job."

As Bob puttered with glasses and bottles, he imparted, "Oh, it still is. Then I'll buy out the old man and make millions, selling watered down Margaritas. But even us opportunist pigs take an occasional time out from our scheming, for a little compassion check. And Marla, my dear, tonight's your lucky night, because you, yes *you* are the sole chosen recipient of that rare compassion we so greedily hoard."

"An honor I'm not soon to forget. Try as I may."

"We'll even wipe the slate clean, and forget about your little attempt at castration. So, step right up, young lady, and tell Uncle Bob all about it. He just happens to have a free shoulder, with your name on it"

"Mighty tempting offer, cowpoke, but I gotta pass. Besides, it's not just about Suz. It's about me. Anyway, this is just something I'll have to figure out and solve on my own."

Bob picked up the whiskey bottle, poured himself another shot, then held up the bottle, as if to offer, which prompted Marla's response, "Okay, but then you're going home."

They drank down the shots, after which came Marla's subdued command, "Now get the hell out of here."

"You sure?"

"I'm sure. And thanks again."

As he prepared to leave, "Think nothin' of it, boss, long as I can be the first to know how the mystery unfolds."

"I promised that to Susan. But second place isn't so bad."

The following morning, Marla's car pulled up close to the front yard of the empty mansion, and stopped behind a late model Cadillac. She got out and stood for a moment, with the car door still opened. Marla stared at Gary, the upscale real estate agent, dressed appropriately in a canary yellow, three piece suit, who stood on the front porch, with his back to her. She wasn't at all happy to see him, but this meeting was inevitable. She resignedly closed the car door and approached the porch, where she jumped up a single step, with, "Gary, hi. You wanted to see me."

"Hello, Marla. Yeah, I, uh, guess you know what it's about."

"I guess I do."

"I'm sorry, Marla, I really am. I wish it could be otherwise, but if you want the deal to close, I'm afraid we'll have to have that money today."

"Yeah, about that money. You see, I sort of – well, I just -- up and spent it all." In an effort to hide her emotion, Marla turned and took a few steps away, as she continued, "Found some other silly whim, went and spent the whole ten grand. Isn't that just like some impulsive female?"

Gary went to her, "I know what you spent the money on." Teary eyed, Marla turned to face him, then stared at the ground, as he went on, "Don't ask me how, I just do. And – are you listening? Marla?"

Still unable to make eye contact, Marla nodded. Gary continued, "You did the right thing. Trust me, you did."

Between sniffles, "Did I?"

"You did. I'll leave you now. Stay as long as you like, and I'll see you again. Okay, Marla?"

She forced a feeble smile and a slight wave, as Gary turned toward his car, leaving Marla alone on the porch.

Thirty days later, after logging countless hours, strapped to a tilt table, concurrent with speech and motor therapy, Susan, by all reports, was ready for her first efforts in the world of upwardly mobile ambulation, aka *walking.* In the physical therapy gym, with a male therapist at her side, and Marla, who needled and taunted her from the opposite end of a portable, double hand rail, Susan struggled mightily to pull herself up from the wheelchair, to a standing position. Cindy sat nearby and quietly watched.

With a frustrated groan, Susan fell back into the chair.

"Loser," Marla casually chided. Suz shot her an angry eyed glare, at which Marla, hands on hips, strolled toward her and continued, "It's no wonder I got no friends. I always pick --" now face to face with Susan, "-- losers."

Susan took a swing at her with the good arm, but Marla ducked away, sported a cynical laugh. She moved back down to the opposite end of the handrails, where she beckoned to her lover and teased, "Come and get me, loser. Come on," and then, in sing-song fashion, "Suzy's a loser, Suzy's a loser --"

As Marla continued the sonnet, Susan again struggled to pull herself out of the chair. When she got halfway up, Marla stopped the noise and, with fists clenched, watched, intently. Cindy rose slowly to her feet, in hopeful anticipation.

One final grunt and Susan stood erect. Marla was elated, "Woooooohoo! Yeah, Baby! Yeah!"

The therapist, with a soothed reassurance, guided Susan along, "Now, take a slow, easy step, Susan. It's okay, just take your time, left foot first. I won't let you fall."

Susan leaned her body to bring the braced left leg forward. Marla broke into a rendition of 'The Hokey Pokey,' as she mimed the song's directions. Susan slowly developed a rhythm, one foot in front of the other, assisted by the therapist.

Later that night, in the sterile confines of Susan's room at the rehab, Marla tucked her in, and, as she brought the edge of the sheet up to Susan's shoulders, "You had a busy day."

Susan whined softly, as she reached out with her good arm. Marla gave her a long hug and a light kiss on the lips, after which she reminded her, softly, "I love you so much," followed by a longer, decidedly more passionate kiss.

Susan, after the kiss, continued to gaze into Marla's eyes, and managed to call her a "Loser."

Marla smirked, "Pretty good for an apprentice. Keep it up and you'll be a journeyman bitch like me in no time." And as she stood to leave, "See you tomorrow for dessert?"

"Mm hmm."

"Oh, I almost forgot. I Got a surprise for you."

Susan delighted as Marla went to the closet, opened it and directed, "Close your eyes."

Susan anxiously obeyed. Marla fished out the folded rainbow quilt, "Keep 'em closed."

At the foot of the bed, she unfurled the quilt, which gently settled over Susan's reclined body. Susan opened her big eyes, in awe at what her lover'd done. Marla continued, "I had it cleaned. They got this rule, you can't bring in quilts you had sex on, without washing 'em, or something like that."

Suz laughed as she once again held her sweetheart close. Marla pulled the edge of the quilt up to Susan's chin, and kissed her lips lightly again, "Sleep now. Rocky Road tomorrow."

A few hours later, alone in her apartment, Marla stood casually at the kitchen sink and washed dishes. Her mind on nothing in particular, she washed, rinsed and washed again, until she froze, looked to her left and listened to the night. With sudsy hands, she took a few guarded steps toward the front door. For her ears only, piccolo music played faintly. Her brow furrowed with curiosity, until she recognized 'Amazing Grace.' As the solo grew louder, Marla got the message, "No – no! Don't you *dare*!"

Marla grabbed her Levi jacket off the couch and bolted out the door. In the parking lot, she quickly unlocked the car door, jumped in and cranked the ignition. And cranked and cranked, until, "Come on, goddamnit!" The engine finally ignited; a determined Marla burned rubber in both directions, as the car backed out of its space, then sped off into the night.

In her room at the rehab, Susan lay flat on her back, still covered by the quilt. A young female nurse entered the room, carrying a small med tray. "Medication time, Susan," said the dutiful nurse, as she approached the bedside.

"Susan?" repeated the nurse, who then shook her lightly and checked for a pulse. Finding none, she backed up toward the door, turned and shouted into the hallway, "Code!"

On a quiet rural road, Marla's car puttered and died as it rolled off to the side. She cranked it repeatedly, but to no avail. It wouldn't start. Marla got out and, leaving the door open, broke into a run. Her plea, "Wait for me. Wait for me!" echoed in the emptiness of the night.

In Susan's room, a doctor, two nurses and a crash cart were huddled at her bedside. The doctor placed defibrillating paddles on her chest and calmly directed, "Clear."

Susan's body bucked under the electrical jolt. Once again, "Clear," and once again her body bucked, but this was a only a medical formality, as the line stayed flat. Susan was dead.

The small town was eerily empty. Now it was Marla's footsteps, at full speed, that echoed, as she ran down the middle of the abandoned main street.

At Susan's bedside, the doctor and nurses remained, engaged

in low key, medical chatter. Out in the hallway, Marla's fast paced footsteps grew louder, until she appeared at the doorway. She panted, loudly, from the exertion, as she hung on to the side of the doorway for support. A lock of hair was matted to her sweat soaked brow, her eyes fixed in the direction of Susan's body. She straightened up and walked slowly toward the bed. Her wind gradually returned as she got closer to the bed. "Baby?"

The doctor tried to block her way, but Nursie, now in the doorway, sternly commanded, "Doctor," after which she motioned the group out with a quick head nod, over her shoulder. Nursie stepped aside and the three strangers left.

Marla sat on the side of the bed. "I'm here now," she said, softly, as she picked up her dead lover's hand and rubbed it, gently, "just like I promised. We got – so much to do."

She slowed the hand massage, as she watched Susan's face, then noticed, "Silly girl --"

Susan's eyes were still in a death stare. Marla closed them, one at a time, as she reminded her, "First you close her eyes." She began to weep, so much so, she could barely say, "Doncha know?"

Marla rested her head on Susan's chest and wept quietly, as Nursie, who'd watched it all, exited the room.

She walked back to her car, in no particular hurry, did Marla. When she got in, closed the door and turned the key, the engine started right up. "Sure," commented Marla, as she slowly drove off. The clunker ran fine, all the way to the front door of Susan's cottage.

Marla stepped out of the car, stood and leaned against its opened door, while she gazed at the front door of the now dark cottage. She then got back in the car and reached for the door to pull it closed, but balked at the return of the distant sound of piccolo music. Marla re-emerged from the car and looked toward the mansion, where a flickering orange light streamed from the tiny attic window. She walked slowly, with her eyes fixed on the attic window, toward the dark mansion. Warily, Marla entered the building through a side door.

She found her way to the giant living room, where the piccolo music now echoed, as it emanated from upstairs. Marla, dwarfed by the hugeness of the empty room, stood solemnly and stared at the staircase that led to the attic where she'd first fallen in love with Susan.

Climbing the stairs, the music grew louder, as Marla got closer to the attic. When she reached the top of the stairs, the music abruptly stopped. Marla watched the small, candle-lit room, from where the music had radiated, then walked toward it. When she reached the threshold of the tiny room, she wasn't surprised to see that, except for the mussed rainbow quilt on the floor, and a candle on a chair, the room was empty. A snapshot rested on the quilt. Marla knelt to pick it up. She brought a hand to her mouth, fell to her knees and began to weep once again, this time at a picture of herself and Susan, who'd happily held the ends of a dollar bill, and declared 'success!' for the flash of an unassisted camera.

"I'm so sorry, baby," Marla pleaded, as she dropped the snapshot back onto the quilt, then continued to quietly cry into her opened hands.

The California sunrise found Marla's car, winding its way steadily up the Coast Highway, mountains to her right, the Pacific Ocean to her left. She pulled into a small, unpaved parking lot, got out of the car and followed a sign with an arrow, that pointed to the beach.

After traversing a sandy incline, Marla stood sullenly at the top of a narrow path that led to the deserted beach. She began to make her way down toward the beach, but stopped, about halfway, sat on the slope, and watched the ocean. After a few quiet minutes of introspection, Nursie seemed to come out of nowhere, and had a seat next to Marla, on the slope. Marla, unimpressed, only glimpsed at her, then returned her gaze to the ocean. "Are you stalking me?" she asked, as she stared straight ahead.

"Too bad about your friend. That's tough."

"Thanks."

"Guess you miss her, huh?"

"Just who the hell are you, anyway? I saw you at the Hard Knox, too. Why are you following me around?"

"Oh, I think you know us both, hun."

"Us? Both? I'm really in no mood to play twenty questions with some old broad who keeps popping up ---"

"Take a look down there, Marla," commanded Nursie, again at the end of her famously short fuse, as she pointed.

At the base of the oversized dune stood Susan, who stared out at the ocean, then looked up at Marla and waved. On the ground, next to Susan, was a beach ball. Marla squinted at the vision, and looked again at Nursie. Suddenly, she got it. "I'll be damned. Nursie."

"What's say we join Susan?"

Nursie stood, held out her hand to Marla and helped her up, after which they headed down the hill. Susan picked up the beach ball and threw it to Marla, who caught and held it until they were face to face. She placed the ball back in Susan's hands, then touched her hair and the side of her face, "You're not dead. It's really you."

Suz smiled, but shook her head no, "We're just your basic, garden variety astral projections."

"We?"

Nursie intervened, "The real ones, like Bob and Lester and all those musicians, are back in the physical world, very much among the living. And one of them still misses you. Terribly."

As Marla looked to Susan, Nursie had to ask, "Can we assume you've finally felt her pain?"

"My poor Susan."

Susan reminded her, "More than Susan. Marc Antony to your Cleopatra."

"Christine to your Van Gogh," Nursie added, "and Robert to your Miss Barrymore. Boy, talk about a believer in lost causes. And I don't doubt she'd do it again."

She threw the beach ball to Marla, who caught it, then placed it back in Susan's hands, "If she doesn't, I will."

"Don't tell us," said Nursie.

"Tell her," said Susan, just before she threw the ball up and over the hill where Marla'd stood.

Marla watched the ball's flight, then asked, "But, how do I --"

"You wanna take this one?" Nursie asked Susan.

"You walk, silly," Susan instructed, "and when you can't walk, you fly."

Nursie nodded toward the hill, "Lotta fertilizer out there, missy. Think you can handle it?"

Marla took a few steps toward the hill, then turned to face them and confirm, "Love beats death."

"Every time," Susan's responded.

"Uh, but no need to test the theory, before it's time," instructed Nursie.

Marla continued up the hill. About halfway, she turned for a last look, but the beach was once again deserted. Back at the crest of the hill, Marla contemplated what she saw on the other side: the cosmos. And to herself, she mused, "Yeah. Fuckin' lotta fertilizer, Nursie."

Where once having been dragged, kicking and screaming, into the cosmos, Marla now spread her arms and swan dove back into the solar system. Her image became tinier as it ascended toward the real planet Earth.

Amid her moment of rebirth, Marla's head and bare shoulders rose above the water surface of a clear, tranquil stream in the country. The first image she saw was that of a foot bridge in the distance, which crossed the stream. She swam a few strokes, then, as the water became shallower, walked upstream, toward the bridge.

After less than an instant, Marla emerged, on foot, from the right side of the bridge, dressed in the business suit and overcoat she'd worn on the day of her suicide. She strolled, hands in coat pockets, to the center of the bridge, where she paused to lean on the rail and watch the stream roll placidly by. The sound of piccolo music in the distance caused Marla to look suddenly to her right, then to continue her stroll in that direction.

In a cemetery, Susan sat on the rainbow quilt, at the foot of a fresh gravesite, strewn with flowers, and played a melancholy piece on her piccolo. As she played, her big eyes never veered from the headstone at the other end of the flowers, that displayed Marla's name, date of birth and date of death. After the last few notes of the solo, she set the piccolo aside and continued to stare at the headstone. She lifted her knees, onto which she rested her arms, and reflected, "I wonder if you heard."

Susan put her head down on her folded arms. Marla now stood behind her, where she softly proclaimed, "I heard. I heard it all." She leaned down, continued to say, softly, close to Susan's ear, "I *will* see you again. And we'll get it right." After a light kiss on the back of Susan's head, "I promise."

Marla turned and walked off. Susan quickly raised her head, confused, "What?" She looked left, right, then left again, at the sprawl of the empty cemetery. As a light breeze mussed her hair, slightly, something in the distance hit the ground and bounced a few times. Susan turned her attention in that direction, and gazed upon a site which further bewildered her. She stood, then walked toward it. After eight or nine steps, she stopped, with her attention fixed on the ground before her. Susan looked skyward for a moment, then stooped to pick up the beach ball.

Ball in hand, she returned to the gravesite, where Old Joe, the caterer, now stood. With the quilt now folded and under his arm, Joe handed Susan her piccolo. They began to walk away from the grave. Noticing the beach ball, he asked, "Where'd you find that?"

"It sort of found me," Susan answered, then tossed the ball upward, underhanded.

As he caught the ball, "A beach ball in a graveyard. That's gotta be a first. Gonna keep it?"

"Something tells me I should."

Now farther away, Joe flipped the ball back into Susan's hands and noted, "Yeah, it's a cinch no one here'll miss it."

In a gesture of friendship, Joe put his arm around Susan's shoulders, then suggested, "How 'bout a cup of coffee and a stinker? My treat."

"Okay, Daddy."

Little Lifetimes

The pursuit of happiness is all we know
To have fun is our only job
If it makes us laugh, we're in for the distance
If it's something to play, we'll give it our all
If it dirties our knickers, wrinkles our shirts or
Causes flocks of birds to take sudden flight,
The desired effect has been achieved,
Consequences be damned

Put one of us in a room
With a straight back chair
Watch the smiles and giggles, when it
Becomes a rocket to Mars and beyond
Put two of us at a Thanksgiving dinner,
See the simple scheme that builds tunnels in gravy

Put any number of us in any chain of events,
Left to ourselves, we'll turn them all from
The somber occurrences you planned
To the pretend world we crave,
And all in the name of hide
And go seek

Phase III

The rebel remains an insignificant slice of Americana. He becomes significant only when joined, side by side, with all the other multicolored slices. A thousand workers, for a thousand jobs, in a thousand cities and towns form the mosaic that is his homeland's proletariat workforce, skilled and non. Where once he openly rejected enslavement by a government or a substance, the idle dreamer now quietly continues to resist conformity amid a world of conformists. He's the new non-zealot, who stands in support of the humane and unpopular; who refuses to give all of himself; holds himself out as superior to no one; is answerable only to himself. Happy to have made it this far, having proved that there IS life after alcohol, as so many of his peers did not, he bears his past with a high regard. Looks, with fond anticipation, toward the future. Unlike those who've stolen from him, lied to or second guessed him into the new century, his own ongoing efforts toward happiness will require no victims. Therein persists only a facet of his rebellious way.

A Best Laid Plan

My task at hand is not to take the inventory of people
I'll never see again, and whose successes or failures
Over which I have no control,
But is to see this year through.
The insanity had been subtle, tho ever present,
And an unwavering influence on nearly every move I made.

An angry, abused, abandoned child, whom even
Old Howard couldn't have helped, clamored and screamed
As it pounded on every locked door, just to be heard,
In whichever way it could.

To have drank myself to
the threshold of death's door
had only been
a symptom of the insanity.

Now I'll have to see to that kid.
This could take some time.

Balancing Act

The drive home is always shorter.
It's mostly freeway fare, the middle lanes are
Clear, an hour before midnight.
The night carries me faster than daylight.
Tiny reflectors that separate the lanes
Fly harmlessly by, at a visually rhythmic pace,
Like a line of bright stars in a black cosmos.
My own personal cosmos, within which lies
My own personal solar system.

It emulates the solar system in which we live,
Relies on the heart for survival,
While the planets rely upon the sun.
Is that unique?
We've all our own solar system
To regulate and navigate in our own chosen directions.
Should the planets that revolve around our lifetime
Fall out of alignment, there's a solution
Not yet considered, not yet enacted, not yet believed.

Our planet assures me, by virtue of her vastness,
She's got room enough for all of us,
Regardless of our truths,

And *no one* need be adjudged, persecuted
Or killed because of them.
Religion, power and greed all continue to do their level best
To bring about the demise of our human race.
No matter how many petitions we sign,
rallies we attend or donations we make,

The powerful will continue to victimize the powerless.
Tho per chance the day arrives when
All our solar systems align
With the purest of intentions of
A contented, productive human being.

On its surface, a simple vision,
While not without its champions.
Get your planets aligned and
Grow your own solar system.
Be the first on your block!
(some assembly required)

For One of the Four

Turn up the lights, make room at the gate,
Grab your belongings, get out of the way.
Call out the dolphins in clear water blue,
Watch them dance on the wave
Of a dream coming through.

The foreman is happy, the workers let fly
With singing and kicking their feet in the sky.
All Muslims, all prophets, all Catholics and Jews,
Can lay down their books,
We've a dream coming through.

With cunning precision, it lights a new path,
It's bigger than we are, this colorful mass.
Chaos gives way to our moment of truth,
We can clear out the lies,
With a dream coming through.

Now up with the rainbow and silence your arms,
Give peace to the children, give healing to harm.
The guns are replaced by an orchid in bloom,
The night turned to day by a dream coming through.

Louise May Meets Memphis Minnie

Louise May lived ninety four years, and endured four wars and three marriages, the third of which saw a fifty first anniversary. She birthed three children, who'd spawn nine grandchildren, who'd spawn five great grandchildren, and counting. At age five, in 1908, she was made to spend a night in the ice house because she wouldn't kiss the cold blue lips of her grandmother's corpse, on open casket display, in the sitting room of her family's home. At twelve, she was sold by her Iowa farm family, to a baker in Watts, California, then delivered to said baker by way of the infamous Orphan Trains of the 1910s and 20s. Following her escape from the bakery, at age sixteen, her travels and shenanigans, from California to Texas to Arizona and back to California, could easily have been the chain of events that once would inspire Memphis Minnie to sing "In My Girlish Days." Minnie and Louise May, after all, were only three years apart, though their paths would never cross.

Except for her brother, the bootlegger, Louise May would never see any of her Iowa family again. She only saw him once, and only because he needed a place to stash a prohibition era load of bathtub gin, while he rounded up buyers in another state. During his absence, however, she had a rent party, drank up half the gin, sold the other half and pocketed the post-rent profits.

At age 90, Louise May reckoned, with scarcely a rueful tone, after relaying the above story, "I guess it wasn't a very nice thing to do to my own brother. But, god, it was good gin!"

One Born Every Minute?

Some nameless company from out of state needs a delivery driver. They don't say, in the classified ad, exactly *wha*t they deliver, but do say they'll supply the vehicle and route. And off I go.

"That job was filled yesterday," explained the interviewer, to your gullible seeker of truth in advertising, "We still have a sales position open, though. And our sales people make a lot more than the drivers."

The nameless company was selling frozen steaks, by the box, door to door. My first day of training doubled as my last day on the job. I rode shotgun with an experienced sales rep, Clancy, in his beat up station wagon that had no heat and leaked a generous amount of blue exhaust into the cab. I would later, to myself, attribute Clancy's discernible insanity, or at least a big chunk of it, to that exhaust leak.

When we were well out of town, ostensibly on our way to an assigned territory, Clancy pulled off the freeway and into a roadside bar and restaurant. He then proposed, "How 'bout a little breakfast before we hit town? I'm buying."

I had a BLT for breakfast, Clancy had three Budweisers. His

driving had been atrocious enough, without alcohol. One can only imagine the possibilities that now loomed.

"Sure you don't want a beer to wash down that sandwich?" he asked, after draining the second bottle.

"No, thanks. Little early for me."

My answer was truthful, if not incomplete. The stock answer I'd been delivering for fifteen years, "No, thanks, I don't drink," had always seemed a tad pretentious.

Back on the road, Clancy still drove like a madman, though no worse than before the beers. Somehow, we made it to the target area, a rural outskirt of Santa Rosa, CA.

"The idea," he explained, "is to catch them outside, you know, raking leaves, washing the car or whatever. We don't knock on doors."

"Why's that?"

"Because we're not licensed to solicit in this area."

"What areas are you licensed to solicit in?"

"Uh, let's see, last time I checked, none. Oh, wait, we can sell, legally, in Fargo."

"North Dakota?"

"Yeah. That's where we're from. Worked our way all the way out here."

"Why didn't the interviewer tell me any of this?"

"We don't like to give away trade secrets until we know you better."

Maybe I give the human race too much credit for logic and balance, but selling from the back of a beat up station wagon, with alcohol breath, at ten o'clock in the morning? I just couldn't see Clancy separating anyone from the forty dollar price of a box of frozen meat. And he had twenty boxes to unload.

To my amazement, he sold them all, with the same sales pitch, one I could never have delivered, in good conscience. "Hey, how ya doing today? Hey, listen, our truck just made a meat delivery to your local market, and the driver was way overstocked, so he asked me if I couldn't find a few buyers and just give 'em to you, wholesale, right off the truck, so he won't have to take 'em back to the warehouse.

"Now, I got T-bones, New Yorks, rib eyes, sirloins and fillets, all in one box, and I'll tell ya what, these steaks will retail in your store for over a hundred dollars, but I'll let you have the whole box for just forty bucks. Or how's this? I'll give you two boxes for just sixty bucks. And these are all grass fed, prime cuts--"

After the first mark had turned us away, I asked Clancy how he expected to sell all or any of the meat, especially with that fairy tale of a sales pitch, before it thawed.

"Hell, I'm not worried," he replied as he studied a road map, "Every deck has four deuces and four aces. We just left a deuce."

Pick a Day, Any Day

Daily slices of your host's less than historical employment history, from within the depths of dead end and semi dead end jobs. If any of this starts to look familiar, do bear in mind the first unwritten rule of authorship: *Ya gotta write about what ya know about!*

On this day, I sit in my car, near the employee entrance of the clothes hanger factory that pays me, until 2:55pm, while I savor the last cigarette I'll smoke before lunch, four hours later. Seems like forever. No ten, or even five minute breaks. Just twenty minutes for lunch, which the management claim is for our benefit. It gives us all a ten minute head start on the rush hour traffic at quitting time. But wait, this is swing shift. How much of a rush hour can there be at 11:20pm? Maybe I'll have a word with the union rep.

Inside, the noise is constant and deafening, like a thousand vacuum cleaners, stuck on high. I pass through the plastic hanger section, en route to my machine. Much quieter in this all-female department, but the invasive, hot liquid chemical odor is the olfactory equivalent of the oppressive noise that awaits me on the other side.

My machine cranks out sixty wire clothes hangers per minute. I slip a long steel bar through the corners of about a hundred of them, as they move out, upside down, suspended by two long, parallel, threaded bars. I hang the bar on a conveyor that dips the hangers into a vat of white paint, then carries them into an oven where they'll dry and eventually return to me. I then quickly bunch and pack them into a box.

"You have to turn out at least five boxes an hour, so you better be fast," the shift supervisor warns.

I'm not tending the machine, I'm an extension of it. An armature that makes the same repetitive movements. Bend, bunch, pack, hang, bend, bunch, pack, hang. All in the interest of transforming perfectly straight, rigid lengths of wire, of equal length, into sparkling new, ready to work, white clothes hangers, wholesale market value: maybe three cents each.

When hired, I was asked to sign a secrecy oath that promised never to share any of their production techniques with other hanger manufacturers. I chuckled to myself, as I signed. How could they possibly have known that I, disguised as a mild mannered hippie, am really a corporate spy? Yes, and I'm here with the sole intent of stealing vital manufacturing secrets and handing them over to the highest bidder, amid what surely must be thousands of hanger manufacturers, on every corner of every town.

Gobbling lunch, back out in the quiet comfort of my parked car, I listen to a left leaning FM newscast. Seems the government is not just content to take aim at draft resisters and war protesters. Now they've declared anyone or anything remotely progressive to be un-American. We, the entire populous of this polarized society, are now forced to take a side. You're with us or against us. Make up your mind. There's no middle ground. If you choose our side, the pay might be low or nonexistent, but you can be sure it's honest work that takes no human lives, and the lunch hours are longer than twenty minutes.

I did, in fact, have a word with the Steel Workers Union rep about those twenty minute lunch breaks. The next day, I was called into the plant manager's office, which is where I'd first learned of their kind efforts to get us all on the road before the dreaded 11pm rush hour. He opened the conversation by looking me squarely in the eye and asking, "Do you like your job?"

Steeped in the belief that a dumb question warrants no smarter an answer, I responded, "Like my job? My God, I love my job!" Loved it so much that on the way back to my machine, gave the shift supervisor my union sanctioned three day's notice.

On this day, in mid May, 1970, it's my turn to open. I stayed in Berkeley last night and hitched the thirty blocks down Telegraph Avenue, into downtown Oakland, at 5am. It's Friday. It'll be busy. Two full bus loads, for sure. I should run off 250 leaflets. Better to have too many than not enough.

I fly around the old office, which is adorned with Salvation Army furniture, cluttered desks, a huge *fuck the draft* poster, and a wall full of left wing literature that covers everything from human channeling conspiracies to a woman's right to choose. I better hurry, first bus'll be here at six. Coffee's on, floor's swept, all of yesterday's garbage is picked up. The rickety, donated mimeograph churns out all my leaflets with not so much as a paper jam. That could be a good omen.

Now out the front door, I trot across the street and down a few doors, where I plant myself at the foot of the Induction Center steps. It's dawn. The short block is eerily quiet. A calm before the storm. But, be assured there's bustle inside the well-lit, multi story building, in front of which I've set up our daily, one person, informational picket.

As I stand alone in the cold, my thoughts meander back to my own very recent induction day. We stood three abreast, did the other two 'registrants' and I, in a small room, opposite the room's only furnishings, a podium and a picture of Richard Nixon on the wall. A uniformed Army officer faced us from behind the podium. We'd been segregated from the larger group of inductees, a policy born out of fear that we'd contaminate them with the ever spreading disease of youthful emancipation from military conscription. Refusals and no-shows continued to climb. The U.S. Attorney's office in San Francisco had a two year backlog of nothing but Selective Service cases. This meant the average indictment for said crimes was taking six months to a year to come down, if at all. Military indiscretions, made painfully public, had fueled an already raging swarm of resistance.

Said the officer from behind the podium, "When your name is called, you will take one step forward. That step will constitute induction into the armed forces of the United States. Army, Navy, Air Force, Marine Corps. Failure to comply with the order will subject you to a possible fine of $10,000, five years in prison or both, for the crime of willful refusal to submit to induction, a felony."

He then called my name. My feet stayed planted. He repeated the speech, to give me a second and final opportunity to comply. Having no luck with me, he moved on to my two co-conspirators, delivered the same, seemingly automated speech, inserting their names where mine had been. To follow the ritual I'd come to regard as my second act of true patriotism, we were led out of the room, and into a much smaller room, where we were interviewed, one at a time, by an FBI field agent. He seemed more interested in talking football than about the issues at hand. Then, after the interview, we three future convicted felons were told, "Okay, you can go."

Returned from the reminiscence, I hear the Greyhound's air brakes around the corner, and watch the big dog make its wide turn from Telegraph Avenue onto 15th Street. It ambles to a stop, a few yards past where I stand ready on the sidewalk. He's not avoiding me, just leaving room for the second bus.

The noisy diesel engine dies, air brakes exhale, door swings open. Civilian clad, unsuspecting, ethnically diverse recruits file out. The sidewalk fills with them. They mill, they talk, they read the leaflets I've handed them.

"You don't have to go," I repeat, as I hand out each flier, "Free coffee across the street. Come on over and let's talk. Don't worry about the uniforms inside, they'll take you any time till nine."

"Is this legal?" one of them asks, as he takes a leaflet.

"Perfectly," I respond. He joins a growing pack of recruits who quietly choose the unexpected option I've offered. They make the turn toward our office, instead of straight up the stairs, into Cannon Fodder Hell.

The second bus arrives just after the last few bodies have vacated the first. The pattern repeats and we get another, even larger group of freedom seekers. But, hold on. A third bus? This isn't right. There's never been three. It double parks beside the first big dog. I shrug off the mystery, position myself on the street, near the still closed door. It's illegal for me to be off the sidewalk, but I don't see any cops. The door swings open. Now, I wait. And I wait. And I wait.

I can hear lone footsteps from inside. Sounds like sandals. They get closer. Then, a twenty-something guy, who wears only sandals and filthy BVD briefs, bounces out of the bus. He holds a big white duck. A live duck. There's a not-so-pleasant odor. I can't tell if it's him or the duck. Must be why they got their own bus. I had a leaflet at the ready, but pull my arm back, upon first sight of the dodge-in-progress.

"Pretty cool, huh? Got my own bus," he proudly proclaims.

"Uh, yeah, very cool. There's no one else in there?"

"Just the driver. Well, we're off. Wish us luck."

"Somehow, I doubt you'll need it. Hey, what's your duck's name?"

"God!"

I'm greeted, back at the office, by no less than thirty men, who sit, stand, read and sip the free Butternut coffee. Many were bussed here for physicals only, not induction. Thus, like a hospital emergency ward, I give priority to the more urgent cases, those for whom this morning's was the last bus ride. They've already had physicals, but they'll get another shorter one, before their swearing in.

"I've been eating nothing but eggs for three days. I heard it doubles the albumin content in the urine, and –"

I have to break the news, "No, sorry, that doesn't work. They'll take you anyway, and test it again after you're in. How's your eyesight? Ever have nightmares? Wet the bed? Attempted suicide? Got any allergies?"

This kid's physically fit as a fiddle. I'll have to bring out some civilian style heavy artillery and, like a lawyer in court, ask a question to which I already know the answer. "Have you ever been a member of an organization that prides itself in mass killing? Would you like to be?"

Thus is the precursor to a Conscientious Objector status claim which has a 98% probability of failure. The good news is that it's a stall tactic, worth another six months, and, should he choose to refuse induction when the time comes, it'll reinforce his convictions. Before he got here, he knew nothing about the option, or even what a Conscientious Objector is. I suggest it with the sincerest hope that by the time he leaves, it'll be his master plan. Why? Because, you see, we're *all* Conscientious Objectors. Wouldn't we *all* rather be without a war, than with it?

Who's next? This guy's a shoe-in for 'sole surviving son' status. Two older brothers, killed in action. They'll offer him non-combatant duty, but it appears he wants to stay home. Can't hardly blame him.

Who's next? 3-A hardship. He supports a wife, two kids and his mother, who lives with them. Why didn't the draft board catch this? I hand him the relevant form and advise, "Go home, fill this out, send it certified to your draft board, get it postmarked it today. Then relax."

Who's next? Divinity deferment? Says he's a minister for The First Church of The Doors. "It's a stretch," I advise him, "Jim Morrison will have to die in order to achieve his reptilian messiah status that might qualify him as a god, and he hasn't done that yet.

"Go ahead, make the application. Worst that can happen is it'll be a considerable stall tactic, and maybe give you time to make another plan. Tell me about your passion for animals. Would that include ducks?"

Who's next? Apprentice bricklayer. His father's business, which is brisk. Dad needs his help, badly. Local Board says it doesn't qualify as a service, vital to the national interest. "Appeal the the decision. Mail it today, certified. Selective Service law mandates that anything you send to your Local Board *must* be placed in your file. Send them a brick."

Who's next? He wants to know if I can get him in touch with that underground railroad to Canada. I can't advise anything even remotely illegal, so the answer's no. Besides, "This is your country too. Don't let those goons chase you out. Be a patriot. Stay here, join the resistance -- it grows more by the day -- and help us put out the fire they started. Now, let's talk about that football knee."

Oddly, he's not interested, politely excuses himself, exits. Gosh, I wonder if one of those pesky FBI operatives has just graced our threshold.

By 9:15 I'm down to the last three guys, including the chap at my desk. One may not suspect it to look at me, as worn out as I appear, but this could be my favorite job of all time. The only job, to date, where I can't wait to get to the front door in the morning. The job that pays me little or nothing, while it utilizes every inch of my passion that once had nowhere to go. I live on about a dollar a day, and love it.

Our donation can is full of dollar bills, loose change, meal tickets and food stamps. I'll put one of the meal tickets to good use for breakfast, after my relief arrives. The tickets are handed out to the guys, just prior to their physicals, for a free lunch at Foster's Cafeteria, a few blocks away, but since they usually head straight home from our office, said ducats are often donated in lieu of a fee.

I finish up with the guy at my desk, call for the next. A short haired guy stands, I beckon him over. I noticed when he wandered in, well after the 6am onslaught, he seemed frightened and alone. While he waited, he flinched every time the front door opened. When we talk, I find out why. He's AWOL. Came home on his R&R and never returned to Hawaii for shipment back to Nam. I can't help him, but I know some people who can. After a few reassurances that he's safe for the moment, I'll walk him down the street, to Military Draft Help, the VVAW (Vietnam Veterans Against the War) answer to civilian draft help.

Lydia arrives to relieve me. Why would she commute all the way from Santa Cruz, a hundred mile round trip, every day, to work here for peanuts? Surely there's a draft help office nearer her home, where she can just as easily find an outlet for her alleged commitment to 'The Movement.' Sorry, Lydia, I really am thankful for your help, and can sure use the break, but something's uncomfortable about your rigid, out-of-place presence in this environment. It all started when you showed up to interview, clad in a business suit that would have qualified you for the secretarial pool at the Federal Building. For now, I'll keep it to myself. My AWOL friend and I will take a walk. Then, I'll have breakfast.

On this day, there'll be no impudent resistance, aimed at the Court or any other established government entity. The time for me to pucker up and kiss some conservative ass has arrived. I'd sure welcome a little liquid courage from the bottle on the floor, in the corner of the kitchen, though it wouldn't do to arrive at the defense table with alcohol breath.

As I exit the kitchen, our unofficial house mother, shouts from her bedroom, "What do you want for dinner?" A statement of optimism, disguised as a question. She believes that all those reference letters on my behalf worked, and that I'll indeed be home for dinner, as usual, rather than en route to a federal detention center.

"Navy beans."

Remotely, I hear her infectious laughter at my ironic retort. I take a final swig of coffee, then head out the front door of the house, to yet another challenge for San Francisco, the city that seems to delight in its resounding defeats of my innocent endeavors. Are my fears of failure based on logic or merely a glint of paranoid superstition? We'll know in an hour or two.

I stand and face the Bench with Scott, my attorney, who makes the impassioned, carefully worded plea to the Court. The audience is packed with supporters I never expected to see here, including Dad, who's taken time off from work and driven his old Mercury all the way from across the bay, to back me up. The Niel Young lyric, "It's so noisy at the fair, but all your friends are there," loops again and again through the 24/7 musical score of my thought procession. It always plays a song appropriate to moment. The rest of me remains focused on the guy in the black robe, in whose hands my immediate future now lies.

After Scott's speech, there's dead silence in anticipation of the decision. A silence that lasts less than a minute, but seems like hours.

Then, from the Bench, "Okay," and another brief silence as he sets the reference letters aside, continues, "I don't suppose there is much good that can come out of a prison stretch. The defendant has satisfied the Court that he's sincere in his efforts to serve the national and community interest, alternatively. I'll commute the sentence to four years probation, conditional, and refer the case back to the probation department for further review and custodial assignment."

Applause breaks out among my supporters in the gallery. I stiffen as the court clerk -- not the judge -- pounds a wooden gavel to restore order; Scott leans over to whisper in my ear, "You got stupid friends."

Back out in the hallway, jubilation reigns among myself, my rag tag supporters and Dad, who's found me in the crowd, put his arm around me and tearfully declares, "Well, son, you did it, huh?"

We hug for the first time since I was a small frightened child. I don't believe we've ever been closer.

I inform the crowd at large, with an emotionally cracked voice, "You're all invited to a party at our house this Friday. Navy Beans and wine for everybody."

On this day, an assistant manager job at Eco Rents, a 'party and sick room supplier,' looks good.

World class oxymoron? My experience in wheelchair repair, and with the disabled, should make me a natural for the vacant position. A position I will grow to hate after the first two hours, and one that carries with it the dubious distinction of the first ever from which I will be fired. The business, owned by a short, beady eyed weasel named Dave, has been known affectionately by the disabled community as "the crip rip." A reference to its 200 to 300% markups on nearly everything sold or rented, from punch bowls to potty chairs.

Part of the job not covered during the interview is that of bill collector. Had dear old Dave been a Mob boss, we could call it 'leg breaker.' In fact, if the delinquent account holders aren't disabled or in their eighties, I suspect he might seriously consider busting a few kneecaps in order to collect payments in arrears.

On this day, I'm asked, "Are you married, son?" by an elderly woman, as she wavers, dizzily, and holds on to the front door of her tiny home. Not because of any medication she'd taken, but because her aged, feeble legs can barely support the malnourished frame they'd once carried with little or no effort.

"No, ma'am," I respond, inching away, after having collected her past due account.

"Well, when you do get married, hold on to her and love her for all you're worth, because when they die, they're gone for a long -- *long* time."

"Yes, ma'am, I'll remember that. Thank you. Take care of yourself."

Author's note: The end came when an unkempt, out of work motorcycle mechanic, who'd come by our house in Berkeley, for an occasional meal and glass of wine, O.D.'d on heroin in our upstairs bathroom. By the time I arrived home from work, the coroner's station wagon was pulling away. How, one may ask, would a totally unrelated drug death get me fired from my job? Seems Dave assumed, after I naively relayed the incident to him, the following day, that since I lived in the house where it happened, I surely must be on drugs, too. My perpetually red eyelids, a genetic, allergic condition, had already made him suspicious. Neither I nor anyone else in the house was using anything harder than weed or wine. And no one, least of all, myself, was aware that the dead guy in the bathroom had been slamming smack. We thought he was just an affable wino. But try and tell that to a rigid businessman, whose most radical concept of overindulgence is an accidental overdose of ex-lax at bedtime.

On this day, a Saturday, I'm reluctantly awakened in the morning, before the sun is up. It's my day to cook and open, after which I'll carve sandwiches, tend bar and buss tables until 5pm. That's when the night help comes in, after which I'll build sandwiches and dinners until nine. Then I'll break it all down, put the food away and drain the water from the steam table. As I throw the switch that cuts the kitchen lights, everything will appear as it was, fourteen hours ago, when the same switch brought the same kitchen to life.

The last time I unlocked the doors of a business before dawn, was at Draft Help. Not yet having been introduced to the liquid love of my life, I'd then sipped coffee all day. Now it's wine I sip all day.

From a coffee cup. Co-workers joke or chuckle among themselves at how, when I have the chef's duty, the daily special is always Beef Burgundy. I chuckle with them, as I'm not ashamed of the underlying motive for this exotic French dish: A gallon of cheap red wine close by, to enhance the zest of the dish, and to soothe your savage chef. By day's end, the gallon jug that sat unnoticed in the pantry, well over half full, for the past week, will be near empty.

There's no lunch or dinner rush on Saturdays, hence, the reason for my one man operation. Usually in pairs, they trickle in, slowly enough for everyone to get served in a timely, cheerful manner. As I stand behind the steam table display of tempting red meats, deli salads and wheat or white breads, with carving knife at the ready, I await a young couple's decision. The musical theme from "You Bet Your Life" parades, note for note, through my head. I put on my best Groucho Marx, flick ashes from the imaginary cigar and remind the indecisive couple to "Say the secret word and win hundred dollars. It's a common thing, something you find around the house."

They're not the first couple I've tested with this mini stand-up routine. Some get it and laugh, most don't. Me and my vino-clouded judgment think it's funny as hell.

At 5pm the night help files in, right on schedule. Two bartenders, two cocktail waitresses, a dish washer and Mary, who will take over on the buffet line till it's time to close the kitchen. She and I have become close friends. We communicate well and share everything. It's refreshing to have a non sexual relationship with a woman who isn't a relative. In the short time we've known one another, Mary and I have formed a bond of closeness that I hope will carry itself for future decades, and into the next century. For now, she's got her eye on Debbie, a ditsy, bi-curious, blond haired, blue eyed server, who has, up to now, led a very sheltered life in suburban Home Town. She is fascinated to learn from Mary that lesbians actually speak English.

By 9pm, as predicted, I throw the switch and the kitchen's closed. Though I've had only three hours sleep in the last twenty four, my second wind kicks in. Mary and I partake in a shift drink at the bar. Like I need one, having killed the better part of that jug in the kitchen. The night's entertainment, an acoustic male duo, begins, as they do every Saturday, by raping a Beatles' standard. The crowd pays them little courtesy, though by night's end, in a more jolly, drunken state, they'll hold these two amateurs in their highest musical regard, as they crazily cheer them on.

"Say what you will about alcohol," Mary waxes, philosophically, while the crowd thickens, "it makes shitty musicians sound good, and helps ugly people get laid."

On this Sunday afternoon, as I lean on the deck railing of Devin's cottage in the hills, and watch the sun set behind the Golden Gate, I embrace the tranquility of these surroundings. It's all so idyllic up here. The loudest noises are an occasional bird chirp or the distant bark of a dog.

To grace the hill directly beneath the deck, Devin's spent the better part of a day planting his yearly vegetable garden, on three level tiers. First tier, tomatoes, second is green beans, third is zucchini. He's meticulously trenched mini irrigation trails throughout the garden. I watch, as a trickle of water serenely finds its way, via the expertly manicured trails, from top to bottom tier. That Devin's pretty handy with seedlings and a shovel.

In less than an hour, I'll trade this tranquility for an eight hour balancing act on the plank of the Blue Bull. They'll all be drunk, shooting off their mouths, just to hear themselves talk. It's the only commercial address in town wherein the customer is always wrong.

"Gimme a shot in a nervous glass."

"Your glass hasn't been nervous for eight hours, Edsel," I mumble, as I refill his ever present shot glass.

When it was nervous, it was a highball glass. And I'm right, he's been here since the doors opened at ten this morning, hording boilermakers, the loudest perpetual voice in the crowd. Edsel, a grossly overweight, fiftyish Neanderthal, with a wife and three kids at home, missed his calling. Given his deep, clear, resonant voice that's somehow survived decades of rot gut whiskey, he might've had a formidable broadcasting career. Just this people watcher's astute observation, kept to himself.

Edsel's bellied to the bar with three other regulars, Glen, Bob and Roy. What had once been a rational conversation between them has regressed to a four player shout-down. While I have no idea what the shouts concern, the simple presence of their voices could easily unhinge me. I promised myself I'd stay sober tonight. That I'd close a little earlier than last night, go straight home and work on query letters to music publishers. But maybe one shot will assist in my tolerance of these saturated rednecks.

After the shot, I find I was right again. The whiskey burns all the way down. Like spinach for Popeye, it gives me the artificial strength I need to deal with them and their boozy chatter.

After the second shot, I'm actually a good natured, good humored guy, interjecting the occasional grin laden opinion.

After the fifth shot, I'm one of them. So, this is how creative types deal with the insufferable? There'll be no query letters composed tonight, but I'll close up early anyway. Though I too now revel in the sour mash buzz, I can't turn out the lights, lock the door and put it all behind me soon enough.

On this Thursday night, Desiree and I have the main bar of the Green Valley country club, all alone. No banquets, and the golfers were all gone by nightfall. All except four middle aged Japanese men, who sit quietly at a table near one of the posts between the picture windows, as if hiding. They play a table dice game I've never before seen. It involves only three dice per player. Whatever this game is, they're playing it for piles of $100 bills, casualy tossed to the center of the table, prior to each individual shake of the dice cups.

Just before he left for the day, as he strolled behind the bar for a soft drink, Darwin, the club manager, had pointed them out, and cautioned me to "Give those guys whatever they want. They're friends of the owner and they fly in, on a private jet from Tokyo, once a month, just to golf here and shake dice. If they want to stay past closing, let 'em."

At around 10pm, the usual mid-week closing time, Desiree is getting anxious to leave, missing her fiancée, who waits patiently for her, at home. With her female room mate.

Now *my* game begins. Desiree informs the quiet, but intensely focused group of Asian dice shakers that it's last call. Time to lock up.

One of them plucks a C-note from the pile in the middle of the table, hands it over his shoulder to her and asks, "Fifteen more minutes?"

She glances over at me. From behind the bar, I'd watched and heard the transaction unfold. Thusly, I bargain, "Give her two and we'll make it a half hour."

Without a thought, he plucks one more bill from the pile, this time looking over his shoulder, smiling at us, nodding in agreement, "Thank you!"

"Oh, thank *you*," comes Desiree's appreciative response.

Back at the service bar, Desiree hands me one of the C's. A slow night for both of us has become lucrative in the wink of an eye, and there could be more.

As I prepare their last round of drinks, I advise Des to "Make this round on the house," and, based on her admiration of her new roommate, I wonder, aloud, "How would your new roommate handle these guys?"

"She'd probably lose her bra before she delivered the round. But I could never do that. My boyfriend would kill me."

I'm curious, "Really? Kill you for looking a little sexier? The front doors are locked, they fly back to Japan in the morning, so who's ever gonna know?"

"He would, because I'd tell him."

"Why? You're not doing anything wrong. It's not like you're two timing him. You just gave the businessmen a little eye candy and made some money in the process. Strictly business."

"No, we tell each other everything. No secrets. Our relationship is based on trust, communication and honesty," she proudly informs me.

"I see. How nice for you."

On this Saturday night, it's busy, our upscale clubhouse bursting at the seems with reunions, receptions and testimonial dinners. After I punch in, Darwin, in a frazzle, greets me in the hall, and directs me to "Go talk to Desiree. She's a mess and I need her on the floor."

"Where is she?"

"In the dining room."

"What's wrong?"

As he continues busily down the hall, "She'll tell you all about it."

The dining room is empty, but pre-set for an impending private function. In a corner booth sits Desiree, who sobs quietly, napkin to her nose. Rags, the assistant club manager at her side, comforts her, as though in the wake of a tragedy.

I sit on her other side, gently hold her hand and ask, "What's going on, sweetheart?"

Seems her betrothed, Rick, the guy who shares everything, and bases his relationship with Desiree on trust, communication and honesty, and Desiree's room mate had both been kind of busy the night before, when she'd tried numerous times to reach them by phone. They were in Reno, getting married. To each other.

On this day, I pour beer after beer, in a booth at the county fair. By the seventh hour, my arm's tired from pulling the tap. Must be careful, they do a 'cup count' before and after my shift. No sampling of the goods allowed here, and I dare not tempt fate. Any cups not accounted for at the end of my shift will be cause for dismissal. My hands shake so badly, it's hard to get the full cup of beer from tap to customer, without spilling half of it. I'll fix that on my break, when I drink my lunch, in the privacy of my car.

The music pavilion is somewhere close by. I can hear it, loud and clear, but can't see it. Rick Nelson and the Stone Canyon Band take the stage. He plays all of his 50s and early 60s hits, "Young World" "It's Late" "Poor Little Fool" "Travelin' Man" "Hello, Mary Lou," one after the other, each to raucous applause. But wait, didn't he lyrically declare, with the song, "Garden Party," after being booed off the Madison Square Garden stage, for daring to perform *new* material, that "--if memories are all I sing, I'd rather drive a truck"? Shouldn't he be jamming gears on a lonely Arkansas interstate?

On this day, following a union referral, I'm being shown the ropes by the owner of Sid's Coffee shop. The name is a misnomer. There isn't a drop of coffee on the premises. In its prime, before I was born, it had been a coffee shop and cocktail lounge. Since scrapping the menu, they apparently kept the moniker for civic sentimental reasons. I thought the Blue Bull was a dive, but this open sewer -- literally, as an open sewer runs under the floor, behind the bar -- makes it look like a cathedral. This, parenthetically, was also the last ginmill I visited, as a customer, prior to my first DWI arrest.

"Lemme show you a trick," the owner interjects, amid his guided tour of the back bar. He then pulls a cigar box from behind the cash register, "I see you're wearing a watch. Put all your jewelry in this box. When they rob you, for some reason they never think to look here."

"*When* they rob me?"

"Yeah, it happens now and again. We're a pretty easy hit, with the freeway so close."

Between the smell and the minute by minute robbery threat, my tenure here is short. Eight hours and gone.

On this day, like Sid's, I brave another union referral, this time with a spike on the class meter. The Daybreak Inn. It's Sunday morning and they've discontinued their Brunch. Ergo, no business. I'm the only body in the bar, for six hours, except when the manager breezes through. I suppose it could be worse. I mean who else can boast of getting paid union scale to watch Daiquiri bananas ripen?

During my seventh idle hour, the piano player, a bleach blond woman, pushing forty, clad in a black party dress, arrives and strikes up a medley of standards I don't recognize. Between songs, she talks to me, through the microphone. I'm the only other heartbeat in the bar, and not even ten feet from her, but apparently it's a requirement that everything she sings or says be amplified.

"How 'bout some requests?" her amplified voice announces to the empty room, as the between-songs arpeggio softens behind her, "Come on, call 'em out."

Reflective on how I was assured by the manager that this lounge was once a nightly packed hot spot, much like Bob's, Sid's and the Blue Bull, decades before I arrived, I wonder why I always manage to hit these mausoleums after their heydays, thus call out "Born Too Late!"

"Ah, so the bartender likes the oldies," she quips to her imaginary audience, then plinks out the song's melody, but doesn't sing the lyrics. And it's a probably good thing. Her matured vocal tones could never recapture the bewildered teen angst of the Poni-Tails.

My shift is over. I'd like to stay and grace the piano bar. Maybe the songstress and I could wind up in one of the 300 empty rooms, then go our separate ways. But I've already got a date. With a half gallon of fruity flavored security that has a bite I crave more than the advances of any lyrical lounge lizard, and my date never poses the threat of saying no.

On this day, I wait tables for a banquet at the Dogwood Country Club, a few freeway miles from Green Valley. It's busy, 'steak in a basket' for 200. I keep up, though with a pronounced limp, the effect of two broken toes, my price for kicking a wall, barefoot, last night. Reason or reasons, unknown.

They liked me as a waiter at Dogwood, offered a plethora of upcoming events, but, even though the money would have been good, as long as his union card said 'bartender,' your snobbish idealist, rather than take a step backwards, would wait, unemployed, for the right call.

On this election day, it took all of ten minutes to train me for poll worker duties. "Ask them to spell their last names, look up the name on the list and cross it off. Then ask for I.D., then ask them to write their name and address on this list. Then we'll give them a ballot and they wait for an empty booth."

I'm the youngest poll worker. The others, a man and two women, are in their seventies, like Mom and Dad. The polling place is in a senior center. They're very kind to me, perhaps because we're all Democrats or perhaps because it's refreshing for them, to be in the company of someone friendly and under sixty.

At 5pm, the man, Clifford, whispers to me, disappointed, "It's a Reagan mandate. Mondale never stood a chance."

With three hours of voting left on the West Coast, the TV networks declare Reagan the winner. Too bad for the local Democratic candidates, as most of their electoral support will now stay home.

On this Easter Sunday, the ten minute drive to work takes me past four churches. All their parking lots are predictably full. It may seem like a lot of churches in such a short distance, until it's understood that this quaint, bedroom community, a small sampling of the Bible Belt, right here in California, boasts of more churches than gas stations and bars, combined.

As I glide past the full lots and the cars lined up to get inside, I wonder why they're only full on holidays. Why never on regular Sundays? Do they all think they'll be absolved of their wrong doings, thereby gaining carte blanch entry into the great beyond because they've logged the minimum required pew time?

Yes, it's cynical, but do note that two years prior to this drive, I called all the punishing gods together and fired them. They've been replaced by one tolerant, forgiving god, who requires no constant worship, won't condemn me to eternal damnation for such perceived indiscretions as masturbation or verbal blasphemy, and with whom I have a steadfast agreement: I go about my life, in pursuit of my endeavors, without causing undue harm to myself or other people, and, in return, I'm granted small miracles. As few and far between as these miracles may appear, they will add up. To what, ultimately, I couldn't say, but for now, for me, it works.

And what, you may ask, does our new, improved god look like? No idea. Could be a doorknob, could be the landlord's dog, or maybe, as I believed in early childhood, the robed guy on the Hills Brothers coffee can. Or, could it look like me? Mystery solved, I'm my own God. I wasn't born a Catholic, a Jew or a Protestant, I was born a *human being,* and I'm all for the betterment of my species. Is this a self indulgent blueprint for survival, on life's terms, absent any anesthetics? Mostly.

One of those outnumbered bars, on the outskirts of the town, is my destination. Another country club. Cedar Park, my final union referral for full time work. This venue is half the size of Green Valley, but its quaintness and closeness to home would seem to qualify it as one of those small miracles. Also, coasting into the lot, reflectively, I must say, as people watchers' hotbeds go, this gig has shown some definite promise.

I find a space in the half full lot, close to where, just a few weeks ago, a satin and lace bride, during mid reception, caught her tuxedoed groom, ass up-face down, in the back seat of a Toyota, atop one of her bridesmaids. The ensuing chase, up and down the aisles of the lot, he on foot, her behind the wheel of the 'just married' car, netted four smashed fenders, a broken leg for the groom, and an attempted manslaughter charge for the bride. Had this been a scene from a farcical filmed comedy, it could not have been scripted better.

After punching a time card in the kitchen and waving hello to Theo, the Greek night chef, I stroll down a dark hallway, past a banquet room that's now empty. Within the hour, said room will fill to capacity with an all-you-can-eat, post church brunch crowd. Theo and Marcus, the Hungarian nighttime bartender, don't get on well at all. They cuss each other out, nightly, in broken English, always emphasizing the curse words, as if to show off new additions to their English vocabulary, and always over the pettiest of matters. Perhaps here would be a good place to put readers in mind, your author would never presume to judge the characters he depicts as stupid, ignorant or in any way, less intelligent than himself, based on their nationality or country of origin. They do, after all, know one more language than I know, which, in itself, gives them a leg up on the comprehension ladder.

"Oh, yes? Well, you can just go and *fuck* yourself! What you think of that, *ass* hole?"

"Well -- you are *cock sucker*! And I hope you die in massive *shit* explosion!"

I fully expect that their inborn contempt for one another will one day escalate to fisticuffs, and, as they're both in pretty good physical shape, can only hope I'm not here to witness it.

Carlos, the Mexican line chef, doesn't swear at anybody. He's overweight, jovial, and knows better than to call attention to himself when he's onto good things. Good things that included the bribing of bartenders, myself included, with a prime rib dinner, in return for two long neck Budweisers.

Perhaps because this business is so close to where I grew up, the banquet room I just passed has been the atrium for more than one trip down my own personal memory lane. I've served a Black Russian to Mr. P, principal of the elementary school, where your promising story teller spent grades three through six. The decades have turned his hair from coal black to snowy white, but, unlike mine, at least it's all still there. He acted like he didn't remember me. He could actually forget someone whose ass he paddled three times?

Same room, different function and a wine cooler for Mr. M, eighth grade wood shop teacher, who, unlike Mr. P, doesn't seem to have aged a day. He remembered me, undoubtedly for the same reason I remembered him. It was in his noisy shop class, on a Friday, that we all got the news of President Kennedy's assassination.

A Margarita for Buddy D. and, by the way, this one's on the house. When asked why, I reminded him, "How could I not buy a drink for the pitcher who gave up the only hit I ever got in little league?"

But the one who struck the fondest memory was one whose name I never knew. A soft spoken, gray haired lady, with a warm smile and oddly soothing aura. During a lull, as I cleaned up, between rushes, she approached the bar, alone, to ask for a refill of her wine carafe. Drinks were hosted for this private affair, thus, no charge, but she laid down five dollars anyway. "Thank you so much," I said, a bit puzzled at the over-tip, “I’m gonna go out on a limb and guess you’re in this business.”

“*Was* in this business,” she corrected, then chuckled and continued, “My husband and I owned a bar in Berkeley for twenty years.”

“No kiddin’, where was it? Maybe I drank there.”

“A little place on University, a few blocks above San Pablo.”

“It didn’t by chance have a fireplace in the middle of the room, with rocking chairs, in a circle around it?”

“Well, yes it did. You remember it?”

“Remember it? I spent one of the happiest days of my life in that bar. Did you ever work the day shift?”

“Yeah, every day. My husband worked nights.”

“Then you probably poured our drinks. Three bourbons and water. For me, Jann and Deborah.

“We’d just come from federal court, in The City. The judge reduced an eighteen month prison sentence for me, down to probation. Jann and Deb -- we all worked together at a draft help office in Oakland -- anyway, they drove me there and back. I could’ve driven myself, but if he hadn’t reduced the sentence, I wouldn’t be driving back.

“So, when we got back into Berkeley, Deborah made a hard left, into your parking lot, and I said ‘What are we doing here?’

"Jann said 'We just thought we'd buy you a drink to help celebrate.' So, in we went. That was the first real bar I'd ever had a real drink in."

"Yup, I'm sure it was me who served it. Small world, huh?"

"And getting smaller. So, why'd you and your husband give it up?"

"Crowds got too rough. We loved the hippies and students. They weren't much on tipping, and we spent most of our time checking ID's, but they never made trouble. Kinda like you and your two friends."

"Uh huh, kinda like us. Thanks for the trip back."

"My pleasure. See ya."

Peculiar thing about that aura. The more I thought about it, the more it paralleled the soothing aura I'd once felt in her rustic little lounge. All those years ago, the three of us sat, drenched in the afterglow of a day's triumph, rocking, silently, as we gazed contentedly into the fire.

And finally, a Coke for Chet, the busboy. At fifteen, he's too young to qualify for a memory lane stopover, but I'd bet I sure crossed paths with his mother a time or two. He was a bright, refreshingly clean cut kid, a little shy, with a family background, atypical of most upper middle class young people.

"My mother was a bartender," he offered, as he leaned on the service bar, after his shift, and awaited a ride home, "You like it?"

"It has its moments, although lately there's usually someplace I'd rather be. Where'd your mom work? Maybe I knew her."

"I dunno, she worked in beer bars, mostly. Topless, I think."

"Ah, so she gave up the biz when you came along?"

"No, not really. I don't know if she ever gave it up."

"She's your mother, I should think you'd know, first hand."

"No, I'm adopted. She was an alcoholic, and gave me up when I was about a year old. She tried to quit a lotta times, so the courts wouldn't take me away. Finally she just told the judge she couldn't do it, and to put me in foster care. She didn't even know who my father was."

"How do you know all this?"

"My foster parents told me. They've been really cool about it. They don't bad mouth her or anything. They just said she had a sickness she couldn't beat."

"Yeah, sounds pretty cool of 'em."

With that, he glanced over at the banquet room door, where a petite, thirty-something woman appeared, clad in slacks and a heavy parka. "There's my mom, gotta go. See ya later."

"Take care, Chet."

They appeared happy to see one another, did the adoptive mother and son, as she gently escorted him out.

I hadn't seen Chet for eight or ten months, when one of the other busboys, who'd usually accompanied him for the soda break, brought me a bucket of ice.

"Where's your buddy?" I asked him, as he dumped the ice in the bin, and I traded him a tall soft drink, "I haven't seen him around for a while."

"Chet? I dunno, man, I don't think anyone's seen him."

"What do you mean? He quit?"

"Oh, yeah, long time ago. But then he got all zoned out on alcohol. His folks gave him a car when he turned sixteen, and he wrecked that. Then he got kicked out of school for drinking, and just started living on the streets.

"He showed up at my house once, looking for a place to crash, but he was all drunk, so I had to kick him out, too. I didn't like doing it because he used to be such a good dude, so I gave him five bucks and haven't seen him since."

"Damn, the kid never had a chance," I lamented, mostly to myself.

"Yeah, maybe not. We all got on his case and tried to get him to stop drinking, but he acted -- I dunno -- like it was out of his hands. Know what I mean?"

"I think I might."

Back in the here and now, I'm opened for business in the main lounge. This day's holiday fare, aside from the usual Sunday golfers' beer trade, will no doubt include lots of Brandy Alexanders and Gin Fizzes, the unofficial Easter drinks, for those whose religion permits it. I'll need more eggs.

On this October afternoon, I hurry to finish the route early. There's one last stop for medical records, in San Francisco. While I could use the mileage money, over the Bay Bridge and back, I'd rather be home early for the first pitch of game three of the World Series. I like both teams, hence, it matters not which one bags the trophy, although a Giants' win, for sentimental reasons of indelible childhood memories, would be particularly satisfying.

Madeleine, my live-in girlfriend, is home today, her only day off from Charge Nurse duties at a local Naval hospital. She, by the by, is a Navy lieutenant. A committed relationship between a Naval officer and a staunchly anti war, former draft resister might seem doomed to incompatibility on its surface. Ironically, however, a far left, anti war, anti government belief system is actually one of the few shared attributes to compliment our intimate bond. The fact that we're close friends, but stink it up worse than spoiled corned beef as lovers, is what I'm convinced will bring about the relationship's inevitable demise.

I'm home by five and she wants KFC for dinner. "Can't you go pick it up, alone?" I whine, "The game's almost on."

"No, I want some company. Come on, I waited till you got home, so we could go together. Please?"

That gives us fifteen minutes to hop back in the car, drive to The

Colonel's, stock up on the most fattening food known to humanity, and be home by first pitch. As an added incentive, Madeleine says she'll not only pay for our dinner, she'll drive.

Mother Earth is a gracious and decidedly enlightening hostess. That we might know balance, she grows her trees on hillsides to point straight up; that we might know patience, she takes a thousand years to poke an island through her ocean's surface; that we might know logic, all of her rivers eventually lead to those oceans. Given the perversions we heap onto her, the pollutants we dump into her, the natural beauty we strip away from her, in favor of progress and profits, she almost never complains. A rare memo from her complaint department, however, can be deadly. Her memos, including, but not limited to volcanoes, earthquakes, avalanches and tsunamis, all have one common factor. As the ground shakes, the lava flows or the tidal wave grows, we, the tenants in her path, are 100% powerless to do anything more than wish for it to stop. Since this is a force of few words, and the memos are intended only to remind us, lest we forget, of who's *really* in charge, the time elapsed from start to finish of their delivery has been, up to now, humanely short.

Madeleine's car is parked close to the side of our house. So close I can't get my body between the car and the house to open the passenger side door. I'll have to get in on the driver's side and slide over. I've been having short dizzy spells, of late, and, as I reach for the car door, I feel another coming on. This one seems longer than the others, until I look skyward, at our old wooden house, which creaks and wavers side to side, and realize, in a panic, this is no dizzy spell. The earth is moving.

Convinced our house is about to succumb and fall over in a heap,

I pull Madeleine away from the side of the car, toward the middle of the driveway. We struggle to keep our footing while the ground continues to heave. "God dammit, stop it!" I desperately command, soon after which Mother Earth's pulse pounding carnival ride rolls to a stop.

Our old house survived. Inside, by way of the only TV station left on the air, we're given first reports that "The Bay Bridge has collapsed, the northbound lanes of the I-880 freeway have collapsed directly onto the southbound lanes, crushing the evening commute between them, and San Francisco is ablaze with out of control gas fires. No word on whether Candlestick Park, with its 50,000 World Series revelers, is still standing."

I try the phone. Not surprisingly, it's dead. Aside from the dead phone, a few things were thrown off shelves, but no major damage. Did I say the phone's dead? Then why is it ringing?

Madeleine answers, listens, then says "I'm on my way. Hey, how did you get through? This phone's dead," and after a few moments, she hangs up.

"Well, what'd they say?"

"It was the hospital. All shore leave is canceled. I have to go in. They're already swamped."

"No, I mean how'd they get through?"

"He just said they have their ways, and hung up."

I pick up the phone receiver, listen for a dial tone. Still dead.

With Madeleine gone for the night, I stay fixated on the TV. The Bay Bridge hadn't actually collapsed, as the first sensationalist news report had claimed, but a section of it did; the Cypress Viaduct section of the I-880 double decker freeway had indeed collapsed onto the northbound lanes; Candlestick Park stayed standing, but did a lot of reeling and rocking; the Series was postponed indefinitely; panoramic shots of San Francisco, after nightfall, were eerily dark from power outages, dotted only by still burning structure fires. Those buildings, the homes, the freeways, that took over a hundred years to create, gone, by way of a fifteen second Mother Earth temper tantrum.

The exact time of the quake had been 5:04pm, the peak of the evening commute. Ultimately, a death toll that could easily have reached the thousands or hundreds of thousands, but never rose from sixty two, was attributed to the World Series, and the millions of people who'd done exactly as I had: left work early, either to be at the game, or at home in time for the telecast. Had I opted to do the work assigned me, in The City, my chances for survival -- the traffic route would surely have included that collapsed stretch of freeway *and* the bridge -- would've plummeted to about forty percent. For the first time in recent memory, I was only too happy to have followed a trend.

On this day, I begin my fifth year with the same medical information retrieval company, shattering the old man-of-a-thousand-jobs record. Both Heather and Ms. Creamcheese, the co-owners of the biz for which I work, have divorced and remarried during my tenure here. Ms. C had been a single girl for a short time, during which she tested the dating waters. Waters that didn't include yours truly. Heather wasted no time in accomplishing the two things she'd vowed, more than once, never to do. Remarry and get knocked up with her second child. Her new husband, incidently, is now my immediate supervisor. He doesn't work the field, never has. He manages it from his office.

The manager's job had first been offered to me. I politely declined. My place is on the road. I log 500 to 800 miles a week, contingent on daily workloads. While I may be in a race with the clock, daily, it's a race run by *my* rules. I don't wear a watch or have a clock in the car, though I always seem to know what time it is. Call it a gift.

My car's not a small, economical model. It's a big economical model. I wanted reliability, protection and, for those 200 mile days, comfort. Everything works. Everything except the alarm that sounds if the keys are left in the ignition after parking and departing the vehicle. During the last warranty covered maintenance, I asked, "Hey, can you guys fix that alarm so it works? I've locked the keys in the car twice now."

"We'll take a look at it."

They may have taken a look, but that's all they did. "Sorry," came the verdict from the friendly, factory trained, expert mechanic, "we can't find the problem. It should be working. You might wanna take it to an auto-electric specialist."

I felt a sudden wave of smart-ass-itis that overwhelmed me, as I inquired, "Hey, just for ducks, I mean, so I'll know when and if the alarm suddenly works, what the hell does it sound like?"

"It's a bell. It rings. You know, like a bell."

Off to the auto-electric specialist I went. He boasted free estimates, which is good, because he couldn't fix it either. He estimated $200 to effect repairs. I'll get used to life without the bell.

As I pull into my first post-lunch stop, a medical clinic on Oakland's Pill Hill, I'm tired, but thankful that, while Ms. Creamcheese tested the dating waters, I was able to test the employment waters, outside this craft, and, after almost drowning, be allowed back, with no seniority or pay scale interruptions.

Regardless of how sick or disabled she'd become, Betty Lou saw to it that her cynical wit remained a healthy, razor sharp survivor. Her least favorite movie was the syrupy Capra classic, "It's a Wonderful Life," partly because of its corniness, partly because, during the holiday season, it seemed to be the *only* movie on every cable channel, 24/7.

"Look, Daddy, every time a bell rings, an angel gets its wings!" she'd mimic, in unison with the young girl on the TV screen, after which, Betty'd occasionally add, "Precocious little bitch."

Comatose from a mixture of morphine and other powerful barbiturates, I doubt Betty Lou was aware that I and one other person were the only two at her hospital bedside on the day she died. The other was a duty nurse. The nurse repeatedly took blood pressure readings, then, without removing the BP cuff, quietly left the room. Moments later, the heart monitor display settled into a flat line, and the single mother of two, who once aspired to dance with Fred Astaire and sing with Frank Sinatra, had drawn her last respirator assisted breath.

I called my sister from the nurse's station. There'd be some time before she arrived, after which we'd go together to break the news to our grandmother that her first born had passed. After a few minutes, I walked back out to my car in the parking lot, where I slid the key into the ignition, but then sat sideways in the driver's seat, with the door opened for more air, and lit a smoke.

All became eerily quiet as I sat, reflecting on the life of the weekend Beat artist who bore me. She'd taken me to Fellini films in Berkeley, before I could read the subtitles, much less make sense of them. She drank to forget all the unrealized dreams she harbored for herself and her kids, little knowing or caring, until it was too late, that the potables only enhanced the failures.

Halfway through the cigarette, a rhythmic bell broke the silence -- ding, ding, ding -- a bell I'd never heard, and not without good reason. It was the alarm that signaled the door was opened, with the keys in the ignition. The alarm, in the form of a bell that no mechanic could fix, picked now to start functioning, all by itself. Always leave 'em laughing, right, Betty Lou?

On this day, what surprises await me? I ask myself this question every day, during the ten minute drive to work. Halfway there, as I pull the car over, just long enough to gather courage, I conclude I'm as ready as I'll ever be, for whatever the day holds in store. My wheelchair bound friends in Berkeley, for whom I'd worked, so many years ago, as a condition of federal probation, had only been physically disabled. They were not crazy or mute or both. They were not a potential danger to themselves or anyone close to them. They were not hitters, kickers, biters, scratchers or throwers of large objects (stereos, TV's, desks, etc.) My latest charges are all of the above.

Tolerance, even for an avowed humanist such as myself, finds itself in critically short supply.

This is an eye opening experience, and one for which I'm not the least bit technically or psychologically prepared. My technical job title is that of 'counselor for developmentally disabled adults.' The reality is that I'm a glorified orderly. I change a lot of diapers. For adults. Forbearance is a virtue, balance, an asset. If someone hits me, I'm only to restrain and caution them, provided they haven't knocked me out, and *not* hit them back. Four of the five females are docile and usually quiet. Of those four, three have asked me to marry them. Presumably, the fourth hasn't asked because she's unable to speak. Should I give it any thought, I might become uneasy at the prospect that, over the past twenty years, the only women who've aspired to have me for a husband are clinically insane. The fifth is a 300 pound mongoloid named Betsy. She's our hitter/thrower. Without warning, she swings, closed fisted, for the jaw or the shoulder. In the event she connects, an evil chuckle, reminiscent of just about any 1980s slasher film, ensues. Speaking of which, Betsy's not to be near sharp objects.

Folksinger Leo Kottke's Pamela Brown was a real life girl whom, as a high school cheerleader, rejected him, in favor of the star quarterback. The girl of the same name, for me, is a twenty three year old strawberry blond, who can't speak or walk, must be spoon fed, and sports a ceaseless, friendly grin. She's the sweetheart of the bunch. Always agreeable, never loud or threatening, Miss Brown can usually be found, quietly studying her two favorite picture books, one on human anatomy, the other on Harley Davidson motorcycles.

One late morning, as the Disney song, "It's a Small World" began, following a string of 1960s pop hits that the group favored, the always reserved Pamela Brown spun her wheel chair around, cheered, waved her arms and made loud, happy sounds that suggested she was happily singing along.

"Wow," I commented to Nora, another counselor, as we watched, "that song sure pushes her buttons. I've never seen her gush like that."

"Not without good reason," Nora replied, as Pamela, in the middle of the room, moved her power chair to and fro, in time with the music, "That song's the only thing she remembers from before her accident."

"I haven't read her file. What happened?"

"When she was three years old, her parents took her to Disney World, and she had the time of her life. After they got home in the afternoon, she wandered into the back yard, alone, fell into the pool and drowned. By the time they found her and revived her, it was too late. The oxygen flow to her brain was cut off too long, and what you see is the end result.

"Have you ever imagined these people as normally functioning adults, like us?" Nora asked.

"As a matter of fact, I have."

"What'd you see for Pamela?"

"Free spirited biker chick, hair down to her ass, t-shirt, black leather vest, maybe a few tattoos. And did I mention an insatiable appetite for sex?"

Nora laughed, "You noticed that too. Yeah, her physical and emotional development may have been arrested at age three, but there's nothing wrong with the girl's libido. It's doing its job, right on schedule."

Memory reverts to Katie, who'd rolled proudly with my parade of unconventional, free spirited peers, thirty or so years ago. Her permanent afflictions had also been brought about by a violent, watery hazard, in the form of a rogue wave, on a Southern California beach. Perhaps it really is a small world.

Of the male clients, only two serve to tip the stress meter. Ricky can walk, albeit with a pronounced limp. His afflictions are birth related. He screams constantly, but never talks. For attention, if the screaming doesn't have the desired effect, whatever that may be, he pushes his forefinger through the corner of his eye, so far into his head, he touches his brain. He's our biter. Before I drive all of them home in the disabled transport van, later this afternoon, I'll have to strap Ricky in extra tight. Last week, he managed to get loose, sneak up behind the driver and take a healthy bite out of her leg. She's home, on disability now. Her sutures should come out in maybe a week.

Alex doesn't talk either. He appears the smiling gentleman, as he daintily touches people and objects. But then, out of nowhere, he gets a running start down the hallway, and throws himself against a wall, hitting it with a force that shakes the building. The trick is to catch or tackle him *before* he hits the wall. My hope is that he never chooses the picture window in the day room for the same ritual. We're two stories up, overlooking a heavily traveled, six lane thoroughfare.

Afterward

With all my jobs and pseudo jobs safely behind me, I presently find that, while I've routinely made light of them, illuminating only their sometimes humorous, sometimes tragic properties, many of them had quietly paid into a fund on my behalf. A safety net, of which I now partake. Actually, I paid into it, but the employers made the contributions, on my behalf. The amount was always such a pittance, I never gave it much thought, except when the opportunity arose to avoid the deduction, which naturally inspired me to believe I'd gotten away with something. A reminder: You can't be older and wiser, without first being younger and stupider. The Social Security Act of 1935 was enacted so that people like myself might have at least some semblance of monetary comfort, in the form of a monthly stipend, during later years.

Those who look back on their lives and say they have no regrets are lying. Everybody has at least one. Among mine would have to be the dodging of that Social Security deduction, in favor of a few more dollars on a paycheck, initially enjoyed, though all too quickly gone. Now, in the year 2020, as I utilize the benefit, I find it's one of our government's proudest achievements. A life saver, to be sure. Not just for me, but for how many millions of Americans who've been where I am now, and been as thankful as I remain for its existence?

An existence infrequently threatened by the same ultra conservative political faction that's worked tirelessly to repeal said benefit, since the year of its inception. And, at present, it looks as though they're joyously closer than they've ever been to realizing their dream. A dream of causing undue hardship for millions, just because they can.

Often here, I've also made issue of my gullible nature. Silly me, I thought I was unique. Turns out, after watching my homeland be voluntarily surrendered to a narcissistic con man, by no less than fifty four million acutely *gullible*, but eligible voters, well, hell, I'm considerably smaller potatoes. The good news, if there was any to be had, is that the not-so-gullible outnumbered the gullible by somewhere in the neighborhood of three million votes. But, through a fluke of the electoral process, what was once our proud democracy, respected the world over, has devolved into a wannabe fascist dictatorship. The remainder of the free world, which once looked to my homeland for leadership, now looks elsewhere, as it wonders what the hell has come over us. I mention this only for its historic properties. 100 years from now, should humanity survive, historians will emphasize *this* period as the most decisive in the rescue or demise of democracy.

But wait, there's more good news. Seems our self absorbed leader, possessed of an attention span, never longer than that of a rhesus monkey, has so incensed the aforementioned 57+ million, that a good portion of them have hit the streets. And the town halls. And the voting booths. And this, friends, is where I, the adamant author, must declare to anyone looking in from east, west, north or south of our temporarily tilted republic, *it wasn't our fault! Please don't blame or bomb us! We don't know what came over us either, but we'll be fine soon! Honest!* How do I know we'll be fine? Because the new generation of American patriots doesn't limit their protests to the streets. They run for office, to replace the autocrats who got us here. Little by little, we'll be back on level ground, until all will be right again. Well, mostly right.

Don't do as I say, do as I did. That is a brief homage, and perhaps an apology for having once naively believed that quietly leading by example could bring about eventual harmony between the individual solar systems of enlightened human beings. My generation made a lot of noise in the late 1960s and early 70s, none of which, to date, I make any apologies for having been a part of. We ignited a resistance movement, which ultimately blossomed into a nationwide movement, responsible for bringing about the end of a ridiculous police action. This accomplishment could not have been brought about quietly. While it's true that over the decades, your seemingly self righteous host has befriended workmates and acquaintances from all levels of the socio-political stairwell, it's also true that he's never lost site of, or grasp upon his core values. Values that defined a generation, and, in turn, a generation that's always known the day would come when it would be called upon to once again bring those core values to bare, thus allowing newer generations to benefit from our somewhat vociferous, though very effective youth.

And finally, friends, when I proclaimed my refusal to become a part of any military to have been my most patriotic act, to date, it's never been my intention to alienate those who would pick up a gun and, as they believe, proudly serve. In point of fact, I continue, when able, to contribute money to veterans' organizations, not out of any sense of guilt, but just because I'm glad they're home. The days of my resistance to military conscription were very different times. The military, due to such unsavory P.R. issues as the draft, Kent State and the My Lai massacre, had become the bad guys. It was incumbent upon unwavering patriots, in all sizes, shapes, ages and colors, to *resist* policies that undermined our democracy.

Then, along about 1990, fearing another Viet Nam-like backlash, our government sold an impending American invasion of Iraq to its citizenry, by way of a Wall Street ad agency. The agency, in turn, floated popular catch phrases such as "Support the Troops," and paraded actors before the Congress, who relayed carefully scripted stories about the oppressive Iraqi government. Before long, our military was back in the good graces of the populous, where it remains today. If this particular military resistant patriot had it to do over, in the here and the now, would he do the same thing? Unquestionably. But that's just me, believing the human race – my species -- has evolved far enough and long enough, to a point where it can settle its differences through peaceful negotiations, without the wholesale murder of its adversaries. To that end, I remain committed, by the virtues of resistance, to a world without wars.

How tragically ironic I find it, that on this, the 53rd anniversary of the Summer of Love, so many nations, large and small, who've fought one another for generation after generation, and whose soldiers march boldly into combat, without ever knowing the reasons, can see fit to continue their bloody, pointless campaigns. They ask their experts, they ask their gods. They claim there's simply no other way. They never asked me.

Printed in the United States
By Bookmasters